ALSO BY TESSA HADLEY

Accidents in the Home

Everything Will Be All Right

Sunstroke and Other Stories

The Master Bedroom

The London Train

Married Love

Clever Girl

The Past

Bad Dreams and Other Stories

Late in the Day

Free Love

After the Funeral

and

OTHER STORIES

After the Funeral

and

OTHER STORIES

Tessa Hadley

Alfred A. Knopf, New York 2023

THIS IS A BORZOI BOOK
PUBLISHED BY ALFRED A. KNOPF

Copyright © 2023 by Tessa Hadley

www.aaknopf.com

Knopf, Borzoi Books, and the colophon are registered trademarks of Penguin Random House LLC.

"After the Funeral," "Dido's Lament," "The Bunty Club,"
"Funny Little Snake,"
"Cecilia Awakened," "The Other One," and "Coda" first published in
The New Yorker; "My Mother's Wedding" first published in *Reader,
I Married Him: Stories Inspired by* Jane Eyre; "Old Friends," based on an idea
from Henry James, first published in *Tales from a Master's Notebook;* "Men"
was written for the Manchester Literature Festival in conjunction with the
Midland Hotel; "Mia" was written for BBC Radio 4; "Children at Chess,"
inspired by a painting by Mary Sargent Florence, first published in
Royal Academy Magazine

Library of Congress Cataloging-in-Publication Data
Names: Hadley, Tessa, author.
Title: After the funeral and other stories / Tessa Hadley.
Description: First edition. | New York : Alfred A. Knopf, 2023.
Identifiers: LCCN 2022026088 (print) | LCCN 2022026089 (ebook) |
ISBN 9780593536193 (hardcover) | ISBN 9780593536209 (ebook)
Subjects: LCGFT: Short stories.
Classification: LCC PR6108.A35 A69 2023 (print) |
LCC PR6108.A35 (ebook) | DDC 823/.92—dc23/eng/20220603
LC record available at https://lccn.loc.gov/2022026088
LC ebook record available at https://lccn.loc.gov/2022026089

Jacket design by Na Kim

Manufactured in the United States of America
First United States Edition

For my lovely daughters-in-and-out-of-law
Alice, Catrin, Izzy, Bella, Zerlina, Debbie and
in memory of Elizabeth

Contents

After the Funeral

and

OTHER STORIES

After the Funeral

AFTER THE FUNERAL, THE TWO LITTLE GIRLS, AGED NINE AND seven, accompanied their grief-stricken mother home. Naturally they were grief-stricken also; but then again, they hadn't known their father very well, and hadn't enormously liked him. He was an airline pilot, and they'd preferred it when he was away working; being alert little girls, they'd picked up intimations that he preferred it too. This was in the nineteen-seventies, when air travel was still supposed to be glamorous. Philip Lyons had flown 747s across the Atlantic for BOAC, until he died of a heart attack—luckily not while he was in the air but on the ground, prosaically eating breakfast in a New York hotel room. The airline had flown him home free of charge.

All the girls' concentration was on their mother, Marlene, who couldn't cope. Throughout the funeral service she didn't even cry; she was numb, huddled in her black Persian-lamb coat, petite and soft and pretty in dark glasses, with muzzy liquorice-brown hair and red Sugar Date lipstick. Her daughters suspected that she had a very unclear idea of what was going on. It was January, and a patchy sprinkling of snow lay over the stone-cold ground and the graves, in a bleak impersonal cemetery in the Thames Valley. Marlene had apparently never been to a funeral before; the girls hadn't either, but they picked things up quickly. They had known already from television, for instance, that their mother ought to wear dark glasses to the graveside, and they'd hunted for sunglasses in the chest of drawers in her bedroom: which was suddenly their terrain now, liberated from the possibility of their father's arriving home ever again. Lulu had bounced on the peach candlewick bedspread while Charlotte went through the drawers. During the various fascinating stages of the funeral ceremony, the girls were aware of their mother peering surreptitiously around, unable to break with her old habit of expecting Philip to arrive, to *get her out of this.* —Your father will be here soon, she used to warn them, vaguely and helplessly, when they were running riot, screaming and hurtling around the bungalow in some game or other.

The reception after the funeral was to be at their nanna's place, Philip's mother's. Charlotte could read the desperate pleading in Marlene's eyes, fixed on her now, from behind the dark lenses. —Oh no, I can't, Marlene said to her older daughter quickly, furtively. —I can't meet all those people.

So Charlotte took charge, arranging with the funeral director, who was willing to give them a lift home in his hearse, and then breaking the news to Nanna, who was affronted but couldn't be surprised by any new revelation of Marlene's inadequacy. Nanna was a tall, straight-backed widow whose white hair was cut sensibly short. She collected old delft and read all the new novels and taught piano: only not to Lulu, who had wriggled and slid down off the piano stool, wanting to press the pedals with her hands. Charlotte practised religiously but wasn't musical, her nanna said. Of course Nanna was grieving too, for her youngest son. Her other sons were a doctor and a dentist, and although she used to talk deprecatingly about Philip's flying, as if it were something rash, like running away to join a circus or a pop group, the girls understood now that this meant he'd been her favourite. Nanna had lost her baby boy and was inconsolable, like a tragic actress in a film. Charlotte and Lulu looked volumes at each other.

At home they fussed around Marlene, who submitted limply to their ministrations; they kissed her and took off admiringly, piece by piece, in reverse order, all the items they'd dressed her in for the day's drama: sunglasses, black chiffon headscarf, royal blue gloves because she didn't possess black, high-heeled black patent-leather slingbacks. The beloved Persian lamb they enveloped again tenderly in its clinging polythene. Then they sat her down on the sofa in front of the television and turned on the children's programmes; Lulu, pressing up against her, stroked her left hand with its wedding ring, which shone with a sober new significance. Charlotte, feeling grown-up, boiled the kettle and made tea in the pot for them all, stirring two teaspoons of sugar into each mug, and a not extravagant dollop of whisky from the bottle, plus extra milk in Lulu's. She got out the biscuit barrel from where it was supposed to be hidden in a high cupboard, by standing on a stool, as usual. Marlene couldn't reach the high cupboard, either, without using the stool. They ate a lot of biscuits and Charlotte made toast under the grill, with its real flames.

Later, their uncle Richard, the dentist, turned up to make sure they were all right, bringing leftover food that Nanna had sent from the reception—sandwiches and coleslaw and Madeira cake, also two servings of jelly with mandarin oranges set in it, for the little girls. The sisters felt a hostility to this uncle which wasn't rational, but based on their sessions in his terrible chair, equipped so exquisitely for torturing them. Now it was Richard's turn to be made uncomfortable. Clearly he didn't know where to look, in the face of his nieces and sister-in-law's predicament, and what he assumed were the excesses of their emotion. His brother's death was an embarrassment: brash and scene-stealing, he thought, like everything Philip had ever done. Not only that, but the black cocktail dress Marlene was wearing—it was the only black thing she'd got—was very low-cut; for the duration of the funeral, the girls had made sure she kept her cardigan buttoned over it. Richard was rather like Philip in appearance—tall and burly and sandy. As soon as Marlene saw him she lunged into his arms, breaking into hysterical weeping. Uneasily he extricated himself. —Now, come on, Marlene. You have to buck up, you know.

—But I've lost everything, she sobbed.

—Well, not everything. You've got your girls. You have to be brave for them.

—I can't be brave without Philip! I can't be!

—You have to look to the future.

—I don't want the future. I want Philip back! I should have thrown myself into his grave today! I wish I was dead too!

Impressed, the sisters exchanged glances, and Richard saw it.

—Isn't it time these girls were in bed? he said severely.

Then Lulu, too, burst loudly into tears, hiding her face against her mother's half-bare breasts, arms squeezed around Marlene's small waist so that she couldn't unfasten them. Richard was out of his depth. Only Charlotte could calm them all down. When he'd gone she looked in the *Radio Times* and found that at 9:25 on BBC1 there was an episode of one of their favourites, *Ironside.* They watched it while eating the ham sandwiches and crisps, snuggled together, as always for the telly, under a wool blanket on the sofa. Charlotte only just remembered not to exclaim, *Isn't this cosy?* Marlene used to put the blanket back in the spare room whenever their father was due home: but now there was no one, ever again, to stop them enjoying themselves. By the time *Ironside* was over Marlene was fast asleep, exhausted by sorrow, snoring lightly with her mouth open and her eyebrows, plucked to a thin line, raised quizzically. The girls crept into the kitchen; Lulu stood on tiptoe to see over the top of the kitchen counter, surveying what their uncle had brought them from the party.

—Nanna sent us jelly, Charlotte said. —In her special best glass dishes, for a treat.

Lulu was small like her mother, and her wide face was pink and creamy as an angel's in a painting, dark eyes set far apart under thick lashes, the mass of her dark-brown corkscrew curls shivering with impatient energy. She took one of the jelly dishes carefully in her two hands, lifted it up over her head, and—before Charlotte had time to grasp what she intended— let it fall deliberately on the tiled floor, where it smashed in a satisfactory splat of red jelly and orange segments. Shards of glass went skidding across the floor and under the cupboards; they heard their mother stirring in the sitting room, but knew she hadn't woken, because she would have called out to them. After a moment's frozen outrage, Charlotte stepped over the mess to smack her sister hard across the face. Charlotte was tall for her age and very thin, with her pale hair cut short like a boy's; her grey eyes were huge and their heavy lids, dropping over her expression like shutters, conveyed her burden of responsibility. As Lulu prepared to break out in wailing, Charlotte shook her urgently by the shoulders. —We have to clean this up, she said. —We'll tell them it was an accident; they're bound to forgive us, today of all days. But we can't ever be naughty again, now that Daddy's dead.

Lulu protested indignantly. —Why not?

—Because then Nanna will adopt us and we'll have to live with her.

This was a sobering prospect even for Lulu.

ONCE THE EXCITEMENT OF THE FUNERAL WAS OVER, THE GIRLS took in the solemnity of their loss. It was shocking, for instance, when Uncle Richard's wife, Hilary, came round, with their other aunt Deirdre, to deal with Philip's clothes. They were sorting out what his brothers could use and what had to go to the Salvation Army; this felt like a violation to Marlene and she couldn't watch, only sat seeping tears in the living room, unable to shake off a dread that Philip would hold her accountable. He'd never been able to stand his brothers' wives, and hated anyone poking around in his wardrobe. There was something unseemly and even gloating in how Hilary and Deirdre were holding up his suits now for judgement, sniffing the armpits of his shirts and even the crotch of his trousers. After a while the aunts forgot to use their subdued voices, and Marlene and the girls overheard Deirdre saying suggestively, *Well, at least he wasn't alone when he died,* although that was the first they'd heard of it. They looked wide-eyed at one another, but didn't dare ask.

Even though their father had so often been absent, a fixed idea of him had given the girls' daily life its particular flavour, they realised now, and they paid anxious tribute to him in retrospect. He may not have wanted them under his feet all the time when he was home, but sometimes he'd tickled them and thrown them in the air, and also he'd brought them cos- tume dolls for their collection, from all over the world. Some of their treats—supper in front of the TV, jumping from the kitchen roof onto a mattress they'd dragged outside, eating condensed milk from the tin—seemed less pleasurable now that they didn't fear his disapproval. They were haunted, too, by imagining the actual scene of his death, whose details were kept hidden from them, like something behind a curtain in a horror film. *At least he wasn't alone.* Whatever beast had felled their father, so fearless and bursting with his life, must have been potent in ways that were also shaming and disgusting. For a while Lulu had to sleep in Charlotte's bed at night, because she could see Daddy's picture when she closed her eyes.

—Don't be silly, Charlotte said firmly, although she budged up towards the wall resignedly, and punched out the pillow which had been scrunched under her head, so that there was room on it for both of them. —He no longer exists.

—He exists inside my eyes.

By the time she awoke the next morning, Charlotte would be pressed, she knew, into the narrow margin of her own bed, while Lulu luxuriated unconsciously in possession of the rest of it, sprawled on her back with her pyjama top twisted under her armpits and her dark curls sweaty, breathing noisily, the fine red vee of her lip drawn up, showing the little baby teeth like seed pearls.

Once it became clear that Marlene had no idea about money, Philip's brothers carried off from his desk all the papers that Marlene superstitiously wouldn't even touch. It turned out that Philip hadn't had much idea about money, either. The Lyonses convened a family conference; there was grim satisfaction in how their nanna broke the news to them. Philip hadn't taken out any life insurance, and there was very little pension: they would have to move from the bungalow, which was the only home the girls could remember, because the rent was too expensive. Philip's brothers would club together to keep the girls at their fee-paying school, but to cover the rest of their costs Marlene would need to go out to work. Deirdre had heard of a job that might suit her, as a receptionist for a doctor who'd gone to medical school with Dennis. Marlene protested to her daughters afterwards, in an uncharacteristic gush of resentment against their grandmother—mostly she submitted meekly to her authority. They were all three looking around with different eyes, already, at the bungalow which had been the shape of their family life so far, and seemed shabbier and sadder in the light of parting. —I used to have it over her, Marlene broke out. —Because she was a widow and I had a husband living. Now she thinks she knows everything.

Her girls consoled her, Nanna wasn't half so pretty or so nice as she was.

Another revelation at around this time—which certainly Nanna didn't know about—was the appearance on the scene, at least briefly, of Marlene's own relatives. Or two of them, anyway, purporting to be her sister and a male cousin, although the girls weren't convinced—and, as they never appeared or were mentioned again, a doubt persisted. Charlotte and Lulu hadn't wondered much about the absence of any family on their mother's side: she wasn't like anyone else, she was one of a kind. Now that absence was filled out with a vengeance by this improbable pair, who had driven down from Great Yarmouth apparently, squeezed into a bubble car. They must have hoped—when Marlene contacted them out of the blue, self-important with her loss, a few weeks after the funeral, to let them know Philip had died—that there was an inheritance involved. *Stuck-up cow,* Charlotte overheard the sister say, as they departed. Marlene had poured tea in the best beige and pea-green china, shaking with the effort of lifting the pot two-handed. *We knew you had to get married,* the sister had said to her. She was a poisonous puffball in a mushroom-coloured trouser suit; the cousin was wispy, with dyed yellow hair and an earring and sky blue nylon flares. It wasn't easy to believe in their connection to Marlene, who cared about appearances and wanted everything to be lovely, was so proud of the way she dressed her girls. They had looked rather like orphans even before their father died, because she went in for *Victorian-style,* as she called it: smocked plaid Viyella dresses, velvet ribbon hairbands, black ribbed tights which shrank in the wash and dragged down on their legs, so the girls were always having to tug them up.

MARLENE'S EMPLOYMENT WORKED OUT WELL. DR. CHERRY WAS much nicer than Uncle Dennis. He was tall and jovial and stooped like an awkward boy, with black-rimmed glasses and shirt collars greasy from his hair; Marlene thought that his wife didn't look after his shirts properly. Because he was so educated and passionate about medicine, he sometimes offended his patients, particularly the old ladies, by dismissing their illnesses too cheerfully; it was Marlene's role to soothe and charm them, and she was a great success at it. She carried over her reassuring manner from when she'd been an air hostess, before she married. Her daughters, when they were little, had loved playing aeroplanes with her, getting her to put on the syrupy, posh air-hostess voice that was a part of her mystique for them, setting out the chairs in rows in the bungalow's dining room, taking turns to bring round beakers of squash with ice cubes, fastening imaginary seat belts for take-off. *Ladies and gentlemen, we're now flying at thirty thousand feet . . .*

But the girls had grown too old for those games. Now they

came to the surgery every afternoon after school, a picture in their matching maroon uniforms: blazers in the summer, gaberdine macs in the winter, felt hats secured under the chin with elastic. Charlotte, with her disenchanted cool look, was disconcerting, her grey eyes the colour of rain or marsh water, her long arms and legs so skinny; she would set to work right away, sorting out the chaos of filing that would have built up by this time, out of sight in the office, behind the reception hatch where her mother presided with such aplomb. Lulu, meanwhile, lay on her stomach on the carpet in the waiting room, absorbedly filling in the outlines in her colouring book, and returning each pencil crayon, when she'd finished with it, to its right place in the spectrum in the plastic wallet. She got up occasionally to sharpen one into the wastepaper bin. It was peaceful in there among the waiting patients on winter evenings, with the gas fire hissing, Lulu's crayon murmuring steadily on the paper, Marlene calling out a patient's name from her list every so often. Of course the girls were always catching some bug or other; their mother protested that Lulu did it on purpose, so that she could stay home from school. Charlotte liked school, or at least liked coming top in her lessons. Lulu hated it, she was bored to death, neither clever nor good at games. And yet she was popular with the other girls; they liked to hold her hands and touch her hair as if she were their pet. She played French skipping with them in the rose garden beside Main House, rubber bands knotted into long ropes around their ankles. Or she folded fortune tellers for them out of paper: *True Love,* or *Better Luck Next Time,* or *Not Lightley!*

Dr. Cherry's Bemstead Heath surgery was miles from their new flat above a solicitors' office in Purley, and they had to take two buses to get home: often the doctor gave them a lift, driving out of his way. And he came in for a drink sometimes, on sleety dark evenings when they all three coaxed him after he stopped the car, Lulu laying her cheek against his tweedy rough sleeve, clinging to his shoulder and refusing to let go, Charlotte hurrying upstairs ahead of the others, to turn on the lamps and the three-bar fire and draw the curtains across the windows of their front room, which looked onto the High Street—fortunately this was only rowdy at weekends. All the heavy old furniture from the bungalow had been squeezed somehow into this cramped little flat, even the piano; their grandfather, Nanna's husband, travelling long ago in the Far East, had brought back a huge sideboard and two awful chairs like thrones, carved in black wood, which stood like a reproach against the psychedelic flowered wallpaper. Charlotte fetched down cut-glass tumblers from the drinks cabinet, and a bottle of ginger ale to mix with the grown-ups' whisky. She and Lulu drank Cokes, which might have a dot of whisky in them too; she put out stuffed olives and salted nuts in little lacquer dishes.

Even after a long day at work, Marlene was in her element at these *intimate soirées,* as she called them—she couldn't really speak French, but she'd picked up the accent when she was flying, and was a good mimic. *Quick as a little monkey,* Dr. Cherry teased her, intrigued and sceptical, sunk rather deep in the low sofa as if he were trying to keep out of sight, although no one could possibly have seen him through those thick curtains, drawn against the night outside. He nursed his drink to his chest with his knees jack-knifed, his eager boy's limbs over-long in that space so crowded with furniture, his face alight with reason and cleverness. Perched on the edge of the sofa beside him, legs elegantly crossed in her sheer nylons, Marlene would smoke Sobranie cocktail cigarettes and interrogate him earnestly about health issues and slimming diets, or reminisce about trips she'd made before she was married, to Paris or Venice, singing snatches of song, waving her cigarette in the air for emphasis. The girls knew all these songs, they joined in too. Their mother would loosen the doctor's tie and ease the shoes off his feet, declare that he was working too hard. *I wish you'd let me have a go at those shirts.* The doctor—resigned and expansive, relaxing into the heat of the electric fire—said he thought they were crazy, the whole family. He didn't know what he was doing here in their crazy world, he added complacently—slurring just slightly, as much from fatigue as from the drink—when he ought to be behaving himself at home. At a sign from their mother, Charlotte and Lulu went down to the High Street with a pound note, getting fish and chips all round.

Later, seeing the doctor glance pointedly at his watch, Char-lotte would announce that it was bedtime, and march Lulu off into the bathroom to do her wee-wee and clean her teeth; if she didn't watch out, Lulu might scamper back into the front room, showing off in her pink baby-doll pyjamas, bashing out a snatch of "Chopsticks" on the out-of-tune piano, screwing up her face comically at the ceiling, waggling her curls and her bottom, making the doctor laugh until Charlotte dragged her away again. The girls slept in bunks: Lulu would push up hard with her feet on the underside of Charlotte's mattress until Charlotte peered down crossly over the guard rail, telling her off. On nights when Dr. Cherry was there they left the bedroom door ajar, not wanting to be excluded entirely from whatever fun was unfolding in the front room. Sometimes the doctor helped Marlene make coffee; sometimes they watched telly, or Marlene put a record on and tried to persuade him to dance. Sometimes the girls woke up to overhear subdued snatches of talk that was not like conversation at all, but warm and sweet and very low, like something bubbling or fermenting, his urging male voice rumbling alongside their mother's fluting, charming, parrying one, the two voices coiling around each other fluently. And they knew when the doctor left, because the closing of the front door at the bottom of the staircase, beside the entrance to the solicitors', gave out a certain twanging noise, subdued but resonant, which reached the girls like a signal, resolving something even in the deep chambers of their dreams.

When Charlotte was in the fourth year, beginning to study for her O levels, Marlene took driving lessons; to everyone's surprise, she was a natural and passed her test first time. She adored the little red Honda Civic that Uncle Richard chose and helped her to pay for, and amazed her daughters, bombing along a clear stretch of road on the way home from Bemstead Heath, checking proficiently in the rear-view mirror; or backing with deft movements into a snugly fitting parking space, swivelling in her seat to look over her shoulder. Hilary and Deirdre could both drive, but Nanna had never learned, and Uncle Richard told it as a great joke that Hilary was terrified

behind the wheel, went for miles out of her way to avoid turning right against the traffic. Now Marlene and her girls could
go on their own holidays, instead of depending on Richard
to drive them to his cottage in North Wales, where there was
no phone or television and usually it rained; they spent the
week playing Cluedo and Monopoly until he came to fetch
them home. Hilary had encouraged them heartily: *So good to
get away from it all!* Yet even after Marlene passed her test, the
girls still heard a male voice in the flat sometimes, rumbling
in the night. How could it be Dr. Cherry, when Marlene had
driven home from the surgery by herself? Yet it sounded like
Dr. Cherry. On occasion it sounded like Uncle Richard.

—It's funny that they still come, Lulu said, —now that she
can drive.

Charlotte instructed her sternly. —Don't you know what
they come for?

Lulu stared into her sister's face, drawing down insight
from it, taking Charlotte's knowledge inside herself and
connecting it to a diagram of a drooping plant, chalked on
the blackboard by a lady doctor, in a special class they were
given once a year at school, excused for the afternoon from
ordinary lessons. Love is the root, this lady had explained,
labelling the diagram in her neat handwriting. Friendship is
the stem and leaves, physical passion is the flower and must
come last. Lulu had heard all about sex in the gossip that
went around at school. But she hadn't until this moment connected it with the flower of physical passion, let alone with
her own mother.

· · ·

THEN, WHEN CHARLOTTE WAS IN THE SIXTH FORM, THERE WAS a kerfuffle at the surgery and Marlene lost her job. Ostensibly, this was because Dr. Cherry's surgery was amalgamating with two others to form a brand-new Bemstead Heath Health Centre, which would not need so many receptionists. But it was obvious even to the girls that there was more to it. Their grandmother paid them a visit, to remonstrate with Marlene and accuse her of *going off the rails.* Didn't her dead husband's family mean anything to her? Didn't she owe something to Deirdre and Hilary, for finding her that job?

—I can find a job perfectly well myself, thank you, Marlene said stiffly, not without dignity.

—We'll see about that.

Then it emerged that Marlene had found something already, beginning the following week, at the checkout in a little supermarket along the High Street: this seemed only to antagonise their grandmother further. It was the first time she had visited them in the flat. They were invited to her house once a month for Sunday lunch, and Charlotte still went intermittently for piano lessons, in a spirit of dutiful compliance, *though there wasn't much point,* Nanna had said. Now the old lady stared around, as if she were taking an inventory of all the furniture that rightfully belonged to her. She held herself very upright in one of her dead husband's carved thrones, with her coat still on and her handbag on her lap: she had refused tea and sherry. Charlotte had made tea, nonetheless, in the beige and green pot, which looked old-fashioned now, and poured it for the three of them, and passed around biscuits. Probably the biscuit plates were Nanna's too.

—I'm afraid for my grandchildren, Nanna said. —When I see the way you live.

—There's nothing wrong with having a bit of fun, Marlene stubbornly said.

Nanna was frozen, offended to the soul. —Is that what you call it? Fun?

—You don't need to worry about us, Charlotte reassured her.

Lulu had just learned to do French knitting. Sitting beside her mother on the sofa, she wasn't taking much notice of the conversation, engrossed in weaving her wool, with a fine crochet hook, around the four nails knocked into a cotton reel: it was a craze at school. From time to time she stopped to peer with one eye, shutting up the other one tightly, down the hole in the reel, and into the interior of the long snake of striped knitting emerging from its far end. —And it's high time you talked to a professional about that one, Nanna burst out, at the limit of her patience. —It's clear there's something missing. She needs help.

Marlene contemplated Lulu in surprise. —There's nothing wrong with her.

—I knew as soon as I met you that you were trouble, bringing bad blood into the family. I'm only glad poor Philip isn't here to know what's going on.

—If Daddy were here, Charlotte argued reasonably, —then Mummy wouldn't have needed a job in the first place.

She had remembered guiltily, however, when she heard *bad blood,* the puffball sister in her mushroom-suit and the yellow-haired cousin with his earring. Nanna shifted her scrutiny from Lulu to her older sister, perched sideways on the piano stool. Charlotte looked nothing like her mother, but wasn't wholesome and substantial like Philip either. She was angular, with apologetic small breasts prodding her polo shirt, lavender-coloured flares sagging on jutting hipbones, colourless limp hair, a rash blooming on her jaw. No wonder she doesn't have boyfriends, thought Nanna, whose other granddaughters, Charlotte and Lulu's cousins, were talented and popular. Charlotte's air of martyrdom was unappealing—and that bustling, precocious way she had, of putting herself forward. In fact, her tragic, heavy-lidded eyes were very like Nanna's own: Hilary and Deirdre had remarked upon it. Yet she experienced her grandmother's gaze, which was the same milky blue as her delft pottery, as a sensation of cold, impersonal in its passing over her as a lighthouse beam.

—And as for you, Charlotte . . .

But Charlotte couldn't bear to hear sentence pronounced. Swivelling abruptly on the piano stool, she turned her back to the room and launched into playing "Für Elise," very badly and loudly, pumping on the sustain pedal like a bellows. She could imagine perfectly, from her piano lessons, her grandmother's expression of long suffering.

MARLENE WAS HAPPY WORKING IN THAT SUPERMARKET, WHICH smelled of onions and stale water leaked from the frozen-food cabinet. The fluorescent lights flickered sometimes and gave her a headache, but the pay was just as good as at the surgery, and she liked the camaraderie with the other women—she had known right away not to put on her air-hostess voice. There was more excitement in the shop than at the doctor's: shouting in the aisles, and sudden illnesses, and shoplifting, even one or two local drug addicts. And once an actual armed robbery, although only a small one, when a panicking shrimpy-looking man threatened them with a bread knife and took forty packs of Benson & Hedges.

Charlotte ought to go to university, all her teachers said. She got as far as filling in her UCCA form, and going for interviews in York and Durham and Warwick; it was the first time she'd ever travelled on a train by herself. She was offered places at York and Warwick to do Sociology and Psychology, but decided to look for a job at home instead. Uncle Richard came round to the flat especially to try to dissuade her, and reported back to Hilary that his niece was a funny sort of girl, bit of a cold fish, very set on her own ideas. —And you've always taken such an interest in their education! Hilary said, brushing out her greying hair at the dressing table, meeting her husband's look neutrally in the mirror, stranding him yet again in tormented speculation. Did Hilary know about his fling with Marlene, or didn't she?

—How could I go? Charlotte said to Lulu. —What do you suppose would happen, if I weren't here to keep an eye on everything?

—I don't know, Lulu said unhappily. —What would happen?

—She can't take care of herself, you know. Like at the

surgery, when she never could grasp the system for the filing. She couldn't have kept that job for as long as she did if I hadn't helped her.

—But she manages at the shop OK, said Lulu. —Working the till, stocktaking.

—Well, goodness me, Charlotte said contemptuously. —Couldn't anyone?

And Charlotte found a post herself soon afterwards, in Resource Planning with the West Surrey Water Board. Meanwhile, one of the Saturday boys at the supermarket had fallen in love with Lulu, and Charlotte disapproved of him. Damian was nice-looking—with wiry dark hair and wide-apart brown eyes flecked with gold—but characterless to the point of oddity. Visiting them in the flat, he sat leaning forward, hands clasped, staring down at his polished black platform shoes with intensity; it was a struggle to keep conversation flowing, around the blockage of his silence. His wordlessness, however, didn't mean he couldn't express his passion in other ways: when Lulu took him into the bedroom, to listen to Culture Club on the girls' Dansette record player, Marlene insisted they leave the door open. But she needn't have worried. Lulu was vigilant on her own behalf, and had taken in, with a fervour that was almost mystical, how the permitted and forbidden areas were marked out on her compact, neat little body. In puberty she'd shed some of the wildness of her childhood, like a domesticated animal losing its high sheen and nervous quiver.

They hadn't seen Dr. Cherry for long months. And then one evening, when the memory of a macaroni cheese supper hung thickly about the flat, and they were watching the latest episode of *Nicholas Nickleby,* he erupted once again into their lives. Charlotte went down to open the door when the bell rang; agitated and proud, she presented him in the sitting room, where the others were still cuddled under the telly blanket. —Look who's here!

The doctor appeared dishevelled and emotional, slightly unhinged, his glasses steaming up from the cold night outside. With just the faintest shade of reluctance—she was so involved in the story!—Marlene turned off the telly. Graham Cherry apparently was leaving his wife and three children; in the meantime he was staying in a bed and breakfast in Purley, round the corner from their flat. Already Charlotte was imagining him married to Marlene, and putting his foot down in relation to Damian; vaguely, in the background to this happy picture, she might herself, at last, be away at university, coming top in all of her exams. They warmed up some leftover macaroni cheese for the doctor, and poured him a stiff whisky; Marlene rinsed through his shirt and socks in the bathroom sink, hanging them over the bath to dry. He sat ensconced among the sofa cushions, in her flowered dressing gown. —How I've missed you all! he said with a tremor in his voice. —It's been awful at home. If you knew how often I've thought about this cosy little place.

—We've missed you too, said Charlotte tenderly. —We missed our conversations.

The succeeding weeks were feverish with planning and possibility. Charlotte sometimes had a qualm lest, if she went away to university, the doctor might be starved of rational companionship, left alone with only her mother and sister to talk to; it would be worth any sacrifice, she thought, to keep him sweet. But for the moment that difficulty still lay in an unknown future, and the present was joyous. On one perfect occasion, the doctor took them all into London to see *Cats;* they went for a hamburger afterwards and then walked in the crowds along the South Bank, past the illuminated GLC building, whose reflection glittered in the black river-water, where the dark forms of boats came and went mysteriously. Marlene was lovely that evening, after a few brandy-and-Babychams, in her pearl earrings and the precious Persian lamb. She was hanging on one of the doctor's arms, Charlotte on the other, Lulu dawdling alongside them, drinking everything in: they were like a real family, Charlotte thought. When they got back to the flat in Purley eventually, and the girls had retired to bed—not too much longer, surely, for these ghastly bunks, absurd at their age—the doctor really did broach the idea of marriage.

Yet unaccountably, on the brink of the future, Marlene hesitated.

—Oh dear, I don't know, she sighed the following evening, when the doctor was absent—partly sulking because Marlene hadn't leaped at her chance, partly cheering on his daughter in a swimming gala. —Just when everything was getting settled. He says he'd want me to give up my work.

—He's a *doctor,* Mummy, Charlotte exclaimed, incredulous. —A doctor's wife can't work in a *supermarket!*

—But I don't mind it. I like to pay my own way.

—You wouldn't need to pay your own anything, once you were married to him.

The doctor was wounded by Marlene's doubt, withdrew his warmth, and stopped coming to see them. Charlotte began going out in the evenings, with an anxious, important face, to visit his nearby lonely bedsit and negotiate the next step with him. They were like co-conspirators. Sometimes she didn't come home until past midnight.

ONE GREY SUNDAY MORNING IN FEBRUARY, THE DOCTOR AND Marlene agreed to a family walk in the Recreation Ground: this felt more like a truce than an end to the war. —I *am* thinking about it, I promise, Marlene had said to Charlotte. —What's the hurry? I don't want to rush into anything I'll regret later.

They were all subdued and chastened in a bitter wind, under a white sky spitting rain, swathed in scarves, pushing gloved hands deep in their pockets. Damian and Lulu hung behind, shoving at each other's muffled shape; Damian whispered amorously into Lulu's ear, parting her springy curls with his long fingers. Marlene did her best to keep up a flow of inconsequential chatter about her friends who worked at the shop: one had a funny digestion, another had sciatica, she wondered if the doctor had any advice for them? He said, *Not really, they should go to their own doctor,* exuding an air of quiet desperation. The path ran alongside a row of seedy municipal pines whose red bark hung down in strings; lolly sticks and sweet papers and caches of dog dirt, with smeared tissue paper, were tucked in among the tree roots; the light was thwarted and desolate. The doctor stopped suddenly dead. —Oh God, this is bloody, he said, not looking at anyone. Then he swerved on his heel and strode off without a word more, back in the direction of the car park, stooping with his head bent into the wind, long legs working like scissors. Luckily they'd come in two cars.

—Well, that was uncalled for, Marlene said, staring after him. —If there's one thing I can't condone it's rude behaviour.

—Wasn't he supposed to be having dinner with us? Lulu wondered.

Charlotte stood staring at nothing on the ground. Beside the path was a steep bank overgrown with tall grass, bleached and stained and flattened by the rain and wind; she struck off suddenly, descending the bank at an angle, up to her knees in grass, stumbling and nearly losing her footing, as if she were wading through water. At the bottom of the bank she stopped with her back to them.

—Whatever's got into her? asked Lulu in astonishment.

It was as if some gauzy and confusing veil was pulled away from in front of Marlene's eyes, and she saw her older daughter clearly for the first time. Everyone had always worried about Lulu, but Lulu was fine. It wasn't Lulu standing there looking so solitary and thin and dejected, bedraggled like a migrating bird blown off its course. —You go on back, she said, handing the car keys to Lulu. —Wait for us in the car. I'll talk to her.

—Really? What's wrong with everybody?

—Just leave me alone, Charlotte said loudly without looking round. —Go away and leave me here. I want to die.

Lulu and Damian exchanged quick glances of comical surprise, but set off obediently, walking back in the direction they'd come, huddled together and faintly huffy—they hadn't wanted to come out for a walk in the first place. Marlene picked her way down the bank toward her daughter and put her arms around Charlotte, frozen and resisting, from behind; she could smell the Anaïs Anaïs that Charlotte had sprayed on her neck. —You know, if you'd got into trouble, Char, she said hesitantly and quietly, just for the two of them to hear, —I wouldn't mind. I wouldn't care what people thought. We'd love having a baby in that flat. I've still got your old carry cot put away somewhere.

In a scornful voice, flat with despair, Charlotte told her not to be ridiculous. She wasn't pregnant. She wasn't quite that much of an idiot. But she allowed her mother, all the same, to stroke her hunched shoulders through the thick winter coat. —Don't worry, darling, Marlene said, making little soothing noises. —You will get over it, I promise, whatever it is. You're young, you've got your whole life ahead of you.

—But I don't want my life. I hate my life.

Marlene was remembering those evenings when Charlotte had gone round to conspire with the doctor in his bedsit, then came home and let herself into the flat so late, with such a guilty, heated, angry, happy face. She had been waiting up for her daughter each time, in her dressing gown and slippers in front of the electric fire, dozing over the local paper. *Well? What did he say?* And Charlotte had snapped at her crossly, frowning, unwinding her long scarf from around her neck. You could smell the cold night air that she brought in with her. *I can't tell you all about it now. It's too late. I'll tell you in the morning.*

. . .

THE DOCTOR MEANWHILE, AS MOTHER AND DAUGHTER STOOD facing certain realities in the park, was on the road for home: his rightful home, with his wife and children. Hardly caring what reception awaited him there, he felt strong enough for anything. He'd awoken out of a fever dream. As if all the years of his education, and all his hard graft in medical school, could have been meant to end in that ghastly bedsit, or in a stuffy flat in Purley! Batting aside a bothersome slide show of images— Charlotte's goose-fleshed, greenish-white limbs, abandoned like something drowned, against pink nylon sheets that had crackled with static—he shifted in his seat and glanced uneasily in the rear-view mirror. There had been an excruciating scene with his landlady. Dr. Cherry had made a few wrong diagnoses in his career: missing the spinal tumour, for example, that had caused one patient's back pain. And he'd sent away with reassurances a child who turned out to have meningitis; that child hadn't died, but hadn't made a complete recovery either. Everybody makes mistakes, the doctor consoled himself, turning on the windscreen wipers. You just have to be strong enough to learn to live with them. The rain was really lashing now. It was coming down in torrents.

Dido's Lament

LYNETTE WAS IN OXFORD STREET, WHICH WAS A STUPID PLACE to be at any time, and especially at five o'clock on a winter's afternoon. It was her own fault. She'd gone into John Lewis after work for a few things she needed, and then she'd tried on some clothes, which she hadn't meant to, and now she was stuck in a crowd of other shoppers and workers, fuming inwardly and shuffling in half-steps, funnelling into the entrance to the Underground. Everybody was hunched, shapeless in down coats, hooded. Sleety frozen rain was blowing in their faces—no one looked up at the Christmas lights. Someone at work had said that one of the shops was pumping out artificial snow into the street, which made the idea of even real snow somehow disgusting. Lynette was tall, anxious, distinctive, in her late thirties, with coffee-coloured freckled skin; her hair was shaved above her ears and the rest of it, dyed bronze and pink, was piled up in a striking bird's-nest mess, into which soft spatters of sleet blew and melted. She was wearing a red tartan scarf with a wool coat she'd found in a charity shop—bright pink, with a big shawl collar; she believed that she despised the clothes you could buy in department stores. It humiliated her to be caught out in this queue, branded with her own plastic carrier, stupid like everyone else.

A man in a hurry came pushing through the crowd from behind her, accidentally striking her hard with his shoulder as he passed, sending her staggering on her high heels; Lynette stumbled sideways, grabbing at a teenage boy hunched in his thin jacket, and then tripped against the wheels of a pushchair, only just stopping herself from falling on top of the child inside it. She was shocked out of her self-possession, her ankle wrenched painfully, the hem of her pink coat dragging in the dirty slush. A small stir of commiseration opened around her: someone helped her to right herself, and the child's mother reassured the child, who began to cry. —No, I'm fine, I'm OK, Lynette said. —Sorry, thank you, sorry.

The people behind them, meanwhile, were pressing inexorably forward. And the culprit who'd pushed her went forging ahead through the crowd, oblivious of any trouble he'd left in his wake. —Hey, you! Lynette shouted at his back, but he didn't hear her, or turn round. As soon as she was steady on her feet she went hurrying after him, furiously pushing herself between trudging individuals, consumed by her rage at this retreating back in its mid-length tobacco-brown coat, which was swinging open in spite of the weather—the man had his hands carelessly in his pockets. Out of sheer stubbornness, Lynette refused to limp on the hurt ankle, wouldn't allow anyone to see that she was wounded. The tearing hot pain, every time she put her weight on it, seemed inseparable from her injured *amour propre*—she couldn't bear the picture of her foolishness, the idiotic ugliness of her staggering sideways, hanging on to strangers. Suddenly she hated this afternoon, this whole day, her whole life. Ahead of her the tobacco coat dipped down the stairs into the Underground and she followed after it, wouldn't take her eyes off it, couldn't forgive it. Something about that turned back infuriated her—its broad unconscious strength, its serene unawareness of her.

They were all funnelled in together again, through the ticket barriers, and she felt for her Oyster card in the side pocket of her bag without looking, so as not to lose sight of her man—he was halfway down the escalator to the north-bound platforms before she got on at the top. She wanted the Victoria, and at the bottom he turned right for the Bakerloo, but she wouldn't let him go until she'd said something and had some acknowledgement from him. So she followed him onto the platform but couldn't see him at first. Then there he was, back still presented to her, forging his way along the platform to the other end; she pressed through the crowd behind him until she was close enough almost to touch the heavy cloth of his coat, could almost feel the heat he radiated, smell the sweet-sour wool. Lynette put out her hand to tug at his arm and make him turn around, to accuse him.

—Excuse me! she began indignantly.

PERHAPS IT WAS AS SOON AS SHE TOUCHED HIM, BEFORE HE turned round, that she knew it was Toby. It wasn't really so extraordinary that she'd followed him all that way without recognising him—she'd only seen his back, and the open, flapping coat had obscured his shape, a black knitted hat had hidden his hair. Anyway, Toby had changed a lot—filled out and become more definitely, heavily, his good-natured self—in the years, nine years, since she'd last seen him. She realised in that moment, to her surprise, that he'd been just a boy when they separated and then were divorced. They had seemed so ancient to themselves in those awful days, so darkened and wizened with experience and bitterness. It hadn't quite occurred to her, in the time since they'd parted—and the parting had been all her idea and her doing, he had just suffered it intensely, with a white, fixed, wronged stare and outbreaks of baffled protest—that he might have had all this growing left in him.

Toby wasn't exactly better-looking now. In fact he'd never really been her type, which might have been part of the problem. He still had that sandy colouring, his nose raw and pink with cold, something naked in his face, knobbed cheekbones and cracked lips, bony forehead; she guessed that his reddish-fair hair had receded quite some way, underneath the hat. But he had more force now than he used to have, as if his bones had thickened and hardened: something unfinished in his face had been completed and closed. At the sight of her, however, his expression cracked open onto such spontaneous, friendly pleasure that it was like a flare against the underground light.

—Lynette! What are you doing here?

A train was arriving: as the crowd surged forward he grabbed her with both hands, hanging on to her sleeves as if he mustn't lose her, smiling into her face. They let the train go.

—The same as you, stupid, she said, returning his smile.
—Living here.

—I thought you'd gone abroad?

—I did, but I came back.

Still hanging on to her, Toby looked around him as if he'd been so busily preoccupied that he'd hardly taken the trouble, until now, to notice where he was. —Listen, this is no good. Let's get out of here to talk.

—But it's hell up there, too.

—Then where are you going to get off? Where is it you live? I'll get off with you and we'll find somewhere for coffee. Or for a drink. It's really good to see you.

The old Toby—the young one—had been very shy. He had had the air of a country boy, which in a way he was: he'd grown up in a dilapidated farmhouse in Gloucestershire, though his parents weren't farmers, they were artists. But now, how worldly he appeared! He seemed to know how to take command of their time and arrange for their pleasure. And if he was inviting her for a drink, Lynette thought, then he had surely forgiven her for the past. He had got over her, just as she'd promised him he would—though she hadn't ever, actually, been quite sure. She'd been afraid he was one of those men who took a mark for life when he was hurt; but that fear had been only her own vanity after all. Naturally, he'd forgotten her. She knew she wasn't ever going to tell him, now, about how he'd sent her flying five minutes ago and she'd come vengefully after him. —I'm meeting friends later in Marylebone, she lied. —I'm sure we can find somewhere there for a drink. I'm free till eight.

On the train there was no chance of a seat. Standing, packed in against each other among all the wet coats, still smiling into each other's smiles, leaning in to confide—Lynette was tall enough to speak into his ear even though Toby was six foot three or four—and swaying together, hanging on to the bar overhead, they talked with a warmth and ease they might not have managed seated side by side. If Lynette inclined against him she could take the weight off her ankle. Anyway, she hardly noticed the pain, she was too full of her performance: confident, forceful, charming. —You've changed! she said to Toby. —I know what it is that you look like these days. You look prosperous!

Laughing, he blushed. So at least he still blushed easily. —I *am* prosperous. Moderately prosperous. Things have gone pretty well, these last few years. Do I sound smug? The studios are getting plenty of work. We've set up a new production company to develop some more innovative projects, we can afford to take a few risks now. And what about you? You look the same as ever.

—Not prosperous, you mean.

—You know what I mean, he said, flatteringly, but easily—as if her looks, and his pleasure in her looks, didn't dismay him now as once they had.

Well, she wasn't prosperous, she said. She had a temping job in admin at the BBC—it was hardly temping, she'd been there almost a year. It paid the bills, although of course in London it didn't really pay the bills. But she didn't care about money, he knew that. She was perfectly happy, she was still singing. Her parents were fine, both alive, both working: her mother was a nurse and her dad, whose own daddy had come from Sierra Leone, was driving for a private car hire firm, he'd finished·with the buses. —And have you married again, Toby? she asked him.

Did she feel the faintest wincing in him then, from his old wound? It was as if a dull bass note thrummed, in his body pressed against hers in the train's crush. But probably she was imagining it, in his face she couldn't see anything but bright openness. —I thought you'd have heard about Jaz, he said. —We've got two little girls, we're very happy.

—I did hear something. I'm so glad you're happy.

—What about you?

—Oh, remember what I told you: I'm not really the marrying kind. Or the mothering kind either.

—Never say never.

—I've got a nice boyfriend, she added, which was another lie, or half-lie—particularly that word "boyfriend," which she would never have used to anyone else about the man she was sometimes seeing, a musician thoroughly wrapped up in his music.

Toby was tactful. —I don't blame you about the mothering. It's good, but it's very messy. Not much sleep.

When the train jolted and he put an arm round Lynette's shoulders to steady her, she imagined that their two bodies, separated by all the layers of their winter clothes, were sniffing each other out, old familiars, remembering each other's nakedness, and all the daily closeness and lusts and shames that, in the comedy played out by their conscious selves, they must pretend to have forgotten. —I've got a suggestion, by the way, he said. —All the bars will be packed, it'll be a nightmare, pre-Christmas. We could go back to my place in Queen's Park and have a drink there instead. More peaceful. I'd like you to see it.

The last thing Lynette wanted was to meet his wife. She could imagine her already without meeting her, she knew what she looked like from Facebook: small and blonde and sparky, flexible from her Pilates, hostile. —Really? Wouldn't I just be in the way? Isn't it the children's teatime and all that?

—Oh, they're off visiting Jaz's sister. I've got the house to myself.

That was startling. How worldly was he, coolly inviting her to trespass on the very ground of his second marriage? Lynette even wondered for a mad moment whether she'd made Toby wicked when she left him, whether he'd learned from her how to have his own secrets and calculate for his own devious purposes. She studied his open, hopeful expression—cautiously, as if she were just musing over the timing of her imaginary arrangements for later—but couldn't catch any flicker of suggestiveness. Probably what she'd concluded all those years ago still held: if she was too complicated, he was too simple. He must think that they could have their innocence back, as if there'd never been anything between them. —All right, why not? she said. —I'm curious to see where you've ended up.

THE HOUSE—A WHOLE HOUSE! HE REALLY WAS PROSPEROUS!—fronted right onto Queen's Park, so that at both ends of the long sitting room, on the first floor, you looked out onto bare winter trees, a tracery of wet branches gleaming black in the reflected light from the windows. Toby went around switching on lamps but didn't draw the curtains, and so the room was filled with their awareness of the thin city darkness outside, and the rushing sound of the rain which had begun to fall in earnest. He knelt to put a match to the kindling in the wood-burning stove. Lynette was taking in the distinctive, comfortable, expensive room, well lived-in, filled with an idiosyncratic mix of old things and modern ones: a worn leather sofa with scuffed cushions, smouldering-red rugs on the dark polished boards, some ancient silk appliqué on one wall, a painted rocking horse, piles of children's books, toys, an elliptical coffee table of smoked glass, Bose hi-fi, shelves stacked with vinyl. Oh, I'd like to stay here, she thought before she could stop herself: she was dead tired, it had been a long day. Toby shook out the match and behind the bleary stove-window young white flames sucked and stretched, as sinuously as animals.

—You've trailed your coat in the mud, he noticed, still kneeling, picking up her hem and frowning at it; Lynette saw with a pang the patch on his crown where the hair was sparse. —We ought to put it to dry, he said. —Then you can brush it off before you go out again.

Pretending to see the mud for the first time, she told him not to fuss, it didn't matter, but he insisted on carrying off the coat to hang it somewhere warm. There had always been a mismatch between the rugged form of him—knotty biceps and big, coarse, freckled hands—and the delicate way he touched things and fretted over them. Lynette remembered that this scrupulous solicitousness of his had goaded her into bad behaviour; it had made her careless and wasteful, afraid that his loving kindness might enclose her too entirely, like a sheath. Left alone in his sitting room, she stood stubbornly without exploring, putting her weight on her good foot, rubbing her long tapering hands together, palms yellow with cold, nails painted dark maroon, in the heat that was only just starting to come from the stove. She heard a reassuring rush of life into the central heating system, which Toby must have turned on, radiators ticking as they began to warm up. When he returned, he'd taken off his coat and was carrying two glasses of white wine, the glass faintly green, stems twisted like barley sugar. She tapped one with her nail, making it ring. —Is white all right? he asked. —You used to like it.

In the old days, he was always searching anxiously in her face to see whether she liked things or didn't like them; his subordination to her will had dragged at her, making her resentful. Now she couldn't see past some new barrier in his eyes, as if behind it he were placid and settled, hardened. —I still do, she said. —What a lovely place.

He glanced around him proprietorially, pleased. —Do you approve?

—You've got your mother's good taste. I don't mean exactly the same taste as hers, but the same confidence and good instincts. I thought I was going to discover things about Jaz when I came in here, but I can't feel her anywhere.

—Jaz isn't interested in her surroundings, just so long as everything's comfortable. She can't believe what a big deal I make out of choosing stuff. She's like you: everything's in the inner life.

Displeased, Lynette tapped on her glass again, drumming a

rhythm, turning away from him to look at an old clock with an enamelled face, painted with dancing cupids, telling the wrong time. —This is a nice piece, she said randomly, though she hated the simpering pink cupids. Why did men always want to do that, run their women together into a continuum? He used to tell her once that she was like his mother, Carol— which hadn't been true in the least, although she'd loved Carol. Had Toby forgotten Lynette so thoroughly, or had he never known her: how could he not see that she and Jaz were opposites, who would dislike each other on sight? In her photographs, at least before she had babies—Lynette had stopped looking afterwards—Jaz was usually huddled with a crowd of similar-looking friends, fellow schoolteachers perhaps, their arms around one another's necks. They were all grinning, and one of them might have her eyes crossed, or be sticking her tongue out, and it might be Jaz; sometimes they were wearing funny hats, or set against the backdrop of a foreign city. As soon as she saw the photos Lynette had understood that Toby had opted for an easier, chummier life, turning his back on certain kinds of difficulty. And why not?

She sat down in one corner of the leather sofa, with Toby at an angle to her, their knees almost touching, in a low chair covered in striped velvet. He had been right to bring her here. In the anonymity of a bar somewhere, they'd have fallen easily into a surface flirtation under her control; here, in his family home, everything was transparent, and therefore went deeper. How could they be strangers now, when they'd been so intimate once? They had belonged to each other in their youth. Her eyes filled with tears unexpectedly, at the idea of

it. The wine was very cold, delicious; her body was relaxing in the thickening warmth of the room, while the clarifying alcohol flashed through her blood like ice. Reminiscing,
avoiding treacheries, she and Toby seemed to be passing on safe
stepping-stones above dark-flowing water. Toby was sorry he
hadn't kept in touch with her brothers: such lovely guys, used
to seem super cool to him. They were a nightmare, Lynette
said: they'd been in all sorts of trouble, but were settled now.
One painting and decorating, one in the police—you know,
poacher turned gamekeeper, what a joke. And how was his
mother? Lynette knew about the cancer—was it still in remis-
sion? Carol wasn't so well, Toby said. She was having more
chemo. Lynette touched the back of his hand kindly, lightly.

—Do you remember our car crash, she said. —On the way
home from your parents' house? When that white truck pulled
across on top of us on the motorway because he didn't see us
in his blind spot?

—Clipped our back end when you tried to accelerate ahead
of him.

—I really thought that we were going to die. And all that
time—while we went spinning across three lanes of traffic—
all that time you were just talking to me very quietly in your
normal voice, telling me everything was going to be all right.
It was very calming. No, that isn't what you said exactly. You
were just saying, *Nothing's happened to us yet. It's all right so far.
Nothing's happened yet.*

—Nothing did happen, Toby stoutly said.

—But we could have died tragically young, like lovers in
a story.

He laughed. —I'm glad we didn't die.

Lynette was watching all the time for any little clue that gave away what was missing from his new life. And she was changing her mind about his looks. The raw sweetness Toby had once was solidified now into authority; he was substantial and sturdy, without self-doubt. In the firelight the wiry hair on his forearms and the down on his ruddy cheekbones had a russet glow: she'd felt distaste in the past for that gingery colouring. Now it seemed like a sign sent up from Toby's passionate, secret life, from which she was shut out. Checking his watch, he worried about her friends in Marylebone. —Though I wish you could stay longer.

—Yes, I ought to go soon.

She was running her finger round the rim of her glass, making it ring out. Why couldn't he guess that those friends didn't exist?

—Tell me about your singing, Toby said.

Then Lynette was flooded with all the anguish that music entailed for her. It made her sick that he knew about certain things she'd rather forget: how ambitious she'd been, and the grand idea of her talent that she'd once cherished and had since discarded. Her voice hadn't been as good as she'd hoped, she had failed to make a career out of it—although she did do some teaching, hourly-paid, and also some examining for the Associated Board. Turning her face away, she presented him with her haughtiest profile. —Oh, that. I'm in a show at the moment. You know I'm superstitious: I don't want to talk about it.

—And you have felt free? You told me that as long as we

were together you weren't free to give yourself over to your work completely.

—Did I say that? How pretentious of me!

She felt a spasm of exasperation that Toby had stored up all the nonsense she'd ever spoken and taken it so seriously. In fact she was guesting in a student production of *Dido and Aeneas,* where Aeneas was got up as the captain of an American football team and Dido as a cheerleader—it worked surprisingly well. Toby didn't know anything about music anyway. Lynette hummed to herself, the opening lines of Dido's Lament, looking around her at the beautiful room. How funny that Toby was so simple and yet his simplicity had brought about all these solid, complicated effects in the real world, these material accumulations and accretions—and children too, the branching out and infinite complication of children. Whereas her own complexity seemed to have had no consequences, it was all wrapped up inside her, she didn't own anything significant to speak of, she had nothing to show for it.

TOBY HUNTED FOR A STIFF BRUSH IN THE UTILITY ROOM. While he worked with it over the sink, getting off the mud from her pink coat, Lynette idled in the spacious kitchen, stroking the dark teak surfaces, rattling the drawers open and closing them—so many gadgets!—and admiring the children's photos and drawings stuck to the fridge and on the cupboard doors. What gorgeous little girls! Finally, holding her coat up to the light, he was satisfied. —You can't see any trace of it.

—Here's my number, Lynette said, scribbling it on a black-

board already chalked with *pasta, Calpol, kitchen towel, black olives.*
—Text me, so I get yours. It's been so nice catching up.

—I'd like to stay in touch.

—I'd like it too.

—You ought to meet Jaz sometime.

—That would be nice.

It was still raining hard, but she wouldn't take an umbrella.
—I don't mind getting wet, she called back from the steps
outside his front door, laughing up at him. —It's lovely! I love
the rain.

They were waving and smiling, Lynette turned to go. And
just as Toby closed the door behind her, abruptly stopping
up the flood of light from inside, she put her weight down
clumsily on her sprained ankle, missing the bottom step and
slipping heavily on the wet stone; sick with pain, she cried
out and grabbed at the railings which ran round in front of
the basement area. Toby couldn't hear her from inside the
house, a man hurrying past with his collar pulled up against the
weather chose not to look round. A pale street light seemed
all but obliterated by the falling rain, tall trees in the closed
park reproached her with their penitential stillness. Everything
was desolation—it was too much. Hot tears of self-pity mixed
with the cold rain on Lynette's cheeks. But she wouldn't, she
couldn't, climb the steps to that front door again, although
she longed for the warmth stoked up inside, the flames licking
in Toby's stove. As if the pain summoned it, she remembered
a scene quite unlike the steadying, consoling stories that she
and Toby had exchanged upstairs. It was when everything was
almost all over between them and she was putting her things

into boxes. She hadn't wanted to take much, only a few essential CDs and clothes. She had pretended to be busy with the boxes but her hands were shaking and she hardly knew what she was packing into them, and Toby's ranting behind her turned back was terrible because it was so uncharacteristic, as if something were broken open and exposed in him, that should never have had to come to light. *Take what you like,* he'd said. *Everything you've ever touched is spoiled for me now.*

TOBY STOOD FOR A MOMENT WITH HIS BACK TO THE CLOSED door, not thinking or processing anything, then returned to the kitchen. He had work to do this evening; he ought to make a sandwich or an omelette and get on with it. He checked his phone and then he noticed Lynette's number written on the chalkboard. After a moment's hesitation he rubbed the number out with a wet cloth, rubbed the whole board clean, rewrote *pasta, Calpol, kitchen towel, black olives.* He washed out the cloth and ran the tap water in the sink, rinsing away the dried mud he'd brushed off her coat, sending it spinning down the plughole.

When he took his omelette upstairs to eat it in front of the twenty-four-hour news, the first thing he saw was her forgotten plastic carrier, tucked underneath the sofa where she'd been sitting. He ate the omelette without tasting anything, not taking his eyes off the TV screen, and then when he'd finished eating he put down his plate and picked up the carrier gingerly, without opening it or looking inside. Perplexed, he stood holding it stiffly away from his body. He'd have liked to bury it deep in a dustbin somewhere outside, perhaps in the next street—only he couldn't do that, in case Lynette came back to ask for it. And now that he'd wiped off her number, he couldn't even text her to ask for her address so that he could post the thing, get rid of it. The item incriminated him, whatever he did. Eventually, he hid it at the back of one of the cabinets in his office upstairs. Toby wasn't a natural deceiver, and he hadn't done anything that wasn't innocent. But it was better if Jaz didn't know that Lynette had been here, in this house, printing her presence everywhere so that it seemed to haunt him wherever he looked. If Jaz didn't know, then he didn't have to think about what it meant.

Jaz called, but he didn't pick up his phone or ring her back, he wasn't ready to talk to her, not yet. He was deliberately not thinking something. He wasn't thinking that he had put together everything important, family and work and home, all so that Lynette could get to visit it some day, and see that he'd managed to have a life without her. He knew that if he held off from thinking that for long enough, then at some point it could no longer possibly be true, and he'd forget he'd ever thought it might be.

LYNETTE MANAGED TO LIMP TO A CHILLY, BIG, EMPTY PUB around the corner, where no one was watching the football on gigantic screens. She bought another glass of wine, which wasn't a good idea because it wasn't anything like as nice as the wine she'd had at Toby's, and anyway two glasses always gave her a headache. Halfway down her drink she remembered the silky top she'd bought because it was reduced, and must have left behind her in his house, still fastened with its price tag in its give-away carrier. She imagined Toby pulling out the slinky leopard-skin print and examining it, surprised by how cheap it was, sorry that Lynette couldn't afford anything better, wondering if it wasn't too young for her. At least he was bound to text her now, as soon as he discovered that she'd left it. She put out her phone on the tabletop in front of her and waited. Would she tell him that she'd hurt herself, and that she was still close at hand? *I'm just round the corner, bit of a disaster, I've done something silly to my ankle.* She didn't know yet, she waited to see what words he chose to use. She might not tell him anything, might not even get back to him at all, in fact. She might just take an Uber and go home. It really was better to be free. Or if it wasn't better, then it was necessary.

The Bunty Club

SERENA WAS OUT IN THE GARDEN IN THE EARLY MORNING, before her two sisters got up. It was the best time. Reflected off the estuary water, the light seemed a blond powder, sifted through the summer air onto grass that grew waist-high, its mauve seed-heads heavy with the dew which soaked her skirt. She dipped to wash her arms in the grass, even her face. Earth smells and the pungency of privet, suavity of balsam, were still acute at this hour, unmingled; shadows were as bold as in a child's picture book; swifts and house martins tracked across the pale sky overhead, shrilling in thrilled anticipation. Everything was to come! This unknown day! The garden was so much more lovely now, Serena thought, than in the past when it was scrupulously cared for. A crimson rambler rose, unmoored from its trellis, had flopped fatally forward into the grass, where it bloomed copiously but mostly unseen; flower beds were knotty with convolvulus and bramble; the dense hedge of blackthorn and holly had grown too thick and high to see over the top. She was alone, enclosed with everything that was enchanting, heated, secret.

And yet the house itself was unromantic: a stolid Victorian villa, built of massive blocks of red sandstone, on a steep hill overlooking a small seaside town. Beyond the house, the road meandered upward past more villas, then dustily through a cluster of old cottages around the medieval parish church, which had a distinguished rood screen. It broke out, above the town, onto headlands grown with gorse and heather, with views of the water all the way across to Wales, before dwindling into a gravelled car park where it ended. Here, on the hill's lower reaches, the old-fashioned hotels and detached large houses had been intended to accommodate a certain sort of privileged, discreet, unexceptionable, unchanging middle-class existence—which had changed after all, because it hardly existed any longer. A number of the houses had been turned into nursing homes. The hill looked across, with a distaste it mostly kept to itself, at the white faux-pavilions of the holiday camp on the other side of the town, which hosted wrestling weekends or heavy metal or evangelical ones.

When Pippa, the eldest of the sisters, ventured out from her bedroom with sponge bag and towel to use the bathroom, Gillian, the middle one, was also venturing. —Beat you! Gillian even said, dashing ahead through the door as if they were still fifteen and seventeen. But they were middle-aged now, and self-consciously aware, as they performed their jokey girlishness, of heavy shelves of bosom under their nightdresses. They had outgrown Fern Lodge, the house that had seemed so spacious and gracious when they were children in it. Pippa and Gillian both had adult children of their own, and careers behind them; they lived in two different northern cities and each owned, jointly with a husband still more or less on board, a big house with an en-suite bathroom for every bedroom. Gillian, who was the most businesslike and got on with things, had grandchildren too. Serena, the youngest sister, was different, she lived alone in London. The three of them were assembled in their childhood home because a week ago their elderly widowed mother had fallen and been taken into hospital. They were taking it in turns, two at a time, to drive the forty-five minutes to the hospital and spend the day with her, although she seemed barely to know that they were present.

Waiting in her bedroom for the bathroom to be free, looking out through the gap where the curtains had never quite met in the middle, Pippa caught sight of Serena drifting in the garden and was irritated—partly because the neglected garden made her feel guilty. If Serena wanted to commune with nature, she thought, she might as well take the secateurs with her and achieve something. Or the strimmer—Pippa had bought a strimmer from Argos last time she visited, though no one had tried to use it yet. Still, the morning was lovely, and she lifted her face to the yellow light and heat that splashed through the curtains' gap, the swifts' ecstatic squalling. Hadn't she made these curtains herself, more than forty years ago? Unconsciously, her fingers sought out a place where thread on the sewing machine had snarled under a seam and she couldn't be bothered to unpick it, too eager to see the curtains' finished effect; the mustard-yellow Laura Ashley print was peppery with age now, faded almost to white. Pippa met her own eyes in the round mirror that hung above the chest of drawers; those same eyes had concentrated on themselves in that mirror once with keen hope, as she painted on her first eyeliner. Now she was in her late fifties, with a craggy plain face—which was partly a relief. At least I've got that over with, she thought. Her love for certain unattainable rough town-boys had been an anguish, she remembered then—surprised, because she was used to thinking of them, if she ever thought of them, with fond condescension, as a bit of a joke.

Gillian, meanwhile, shuddered in the bathroom at dubious flecks and stains and gritty surfaces, the yellowed toilet brush clogged with paper, the packets of laxatives and Tena lady-pads out on unapologetic show. Their mother had a cleaner, but she wasn't much good; Gillian and Pippa had worked up quite a head of indignant steam, uncovering her dirty secrets round the house. Sincerely Gillian had meant, on her days off from hospital visits, to give the whole house a deep clean, and then was taken aback by the depth of her own reluctance to tackle it—but why should she, after all, if the others didn't care? Instead she'd trekked sturdily in the sunshine, pleased with herself, three miles each way along the coastal path, in the expensive boots and walking poles she'd bought last year for a holiday in the Lake District, taken without her husband and with a woman-friend. In the bathroom now, she made do fastidiously with standing on one clean towel and drying herself with another. How long, actually, since their mother had a proper bath? She wouldn't hear of installing a shower, and yet Gillian herself didn't find it easy to climb in and out of the deep tub, its enamel dulled to grey by the innumerable baths the family had run in it over the years. Such thunderous floods of hot water, walls and mirror dripping time and again from the steam; such intimate smells, pleasant and unpleasant; such fun, the bubble baths and slippery, screaming games, swimming and pouring and gulping, sucking on face flannels; then, later, such secret longings and excitement and dread, solitary behind the locked door, hair dye and Tampax and vomiting, girl-flesh burgeoning out of control. Thank goodness all that was over.

—All clear! she hallooed when she had finished, popping her head, dowager-like in its wrapped towel, around the door to Pippa's room. Gillian was quicker and lighter on her feet than her older sister, worked harder on her appearance; she had her grey hair chopped stylishly short, and favoured dangly big earrings. Pippa was bookish where Gillian was capable; she wore her hair pinned up, or in a long plait braided on one shoulder, which someone had said once—long ago, when it was still rich chestnut brown—made her look like an Augustus John gypsy. Still, you could see the two sisters' close likeness: they were big and broad-shouldered like their father, with forthright open pink faces, long flat cheeks, an obstinate set jaw. Both sisters had recently retired. Gillian had done something high up in management for the National Grid, and her husband had a business making thermostats for heating systems. Pippa's husband worked on the eighteenth century in the History department at Leeds University; she'd been the director of an archive at the city museum.

—Bathroom's empty! Gillian said. —You should get in quickly before Serena embarks on any aromatherapy. I wish she'd wash the bath out when she's finished.

—She's up already, Pippa said. —Look! Worshipping in the garden.

Gillian came to stand beside her. They were spying, and meant to say something dry and funny about their sister, taking advantage of watching her unseen: dancing in the long grass, flitting like a sprite in her black cotton tiered skirt and satiny top—which she'd most likely got from a charity shop, because she was solemn about waste and recycling. Serena was seven years younger than Gillian, an afterthought in the family, their father's favourite, fey and fine-boned; she'd had whatever success she wanted with the town-boys, and disdained it. She exasperated Pippa and Gillian because she was intolerant and touchy and had no sense of humour; everyone trod around Serena carefully. As a newborn baby she'd been very sick, with a hole in her heart; their father, who was headmaster of the local secondary school, and a lay preacher in the C of E, had prayed over her cot in the intensive care ward, begging God to save her. No doubt that had affected her character.

She lifted her bare feet high and thrust out her arms and Gillian said that she was doing t'ai chi. Serena must have heard them murmuring because she turned her face up toward the window and smiled at them, without interrupting the stately sequence of her moves, and they thought that she wasn't as pretty as she used to be: in the strong light she was drawn and faded, her arms and neck skinny. Her sisters were ambushed then by a sadness that mostly evaded them, in spite of the fact that they were here in their old home, waiting most probably for their mother to die, and for the end of their past. Sadness made its claim on them now, winding through all the daily clutter like a cool long note played on a flute.

IT WAS PIPPA'S TURN TO STAY BEHIND, WHILE GILLIAN AND Serena drove off to their vigil at the hospital. She got out the strimmer from its box and read the instructions, but recoiled from actually attempting to use it, all that crude noise and violence erupting into the peace of the empty house and garden. There was no hurry anyway. The others wouldn't be back till late afternoon—she had all day to cut the grass and make something for supper. Wandering around the downstairs rooms stuffy with heat, in a light thick with dust motes, blinds at the windows lowered to half-mast as they always were in summer, she pressed down keys—startling herself out of her own reverie—on the out-of-tune piano, which none of them had played with any talent.

In the years since their father died, their mother, Evelyn, hadn't changed anything in these rooms—less out of respect than out of indifference. The old-fashioned good taste and extreme orderliness had been their father's idea, it turned out, and not hers. Gradually after he'd gone the place had filled up untidily with her fads—oil painting for a while, then weaving, then the University of the Third Age. Photographs of the grandchildren and great-grandchildren and the cleaner's grandchildren were propped at random behind ornaments on the drawing-room mantelpiece; there were sacks of birdseed on the teak sideboard in the dining room. Also, she'd stopped attending church. She'd surprised Pippa recently by insisting that what she'd wanted all her life was to run a farm, though of course that possibility had never seriously arisen—Evelyn's father's farm, adjoining the edge of the moor above the town, had been passed on without even any discussion, through the male line, to her brother first and then to her brother's son. Anyway, she had always been vague and shy, with a muted irony, flat-chested and thin and awkwardly elegant—you couldn't imagine her in caked boots in the muck, or castrating lambs, or perched high in the driver's seat of a tractor. Pippa was made uncomfortable by these eruptions of her mother's veiled feminist protest, gauche and faintly theatrical, coming so much too late.

Wandering upstairs to her bedroom, Pippa checked the emails on her phone, then succumbed to the desire to lie down again on the bed, with her George Eliot novel. She couldn't remember the last time she had lain down to read during the day—it was like being a teenager, time stretching out voluptuously in all directions. Dreamily, she even half-imagined hearing her mother at work downstairs, a consoling clatter of pans and crockery in the kitchen, water running in the sink, voices rumbling on the radio—as if some substratum of ordinariness were so fundamental that it must always be flowing on steadily somewhere, below all the agitation of change. Although Pippa had sometimes asked herself: What had their mother actually done all day, when she was keeping house? She had seemed so perpetually worn out and preoccupied, yet she'd always had help with the cleaning and ironing, wasn't much of a cook, disliked entertaining, had never worked outside the home. Pippa and Gillian had managed bigger households more robustly alongside full-time jobs.

Then Pippa was absorbed in Maggie Tulliver's forbidden meetings in the Red Deeps with Philip Wakem, her efforts to love him. Pippa urged her on—love him!—though she'd read the book many times before, and knew what must happen. Wouldn't twisted, wounded, intelligent Philip make a far superior lover, however, to handsome, conventional Stephen, and shouldn't George Eliot of all people know it? Eventually Pippa fell asleep, Maggie's travails merging with her own. She only woke hours later, in the early afternoon, when someone rang the doorbell. With a stale mouth and foggy head she struggled up and hurried downstairs, pinning back escaped strands of hair, feeling caught out in idleness, blinking in the confusing shadows of the hall. Its tiled floor was dazzling, spattered with ruby and emerald and topaz light, beamed through the stained-glass picture-panels in the porch door—a heron among green reeds, a kingfisher beside a stream, a swan on its nest.

When she opened the door, a man in a sleeveless orange vest and shorts and ragged trainers was lounging back on one leg against a porch-post, chewing, his other knee angled up in front of him. He spat out his gum apologetically and held out a hand, said he was Sean, a friend of Evelyn's, come to ask after her. He was lanky and rangy, good-looking, burned very brown by the sun. Although he arranged his face to be exaggeratedly solicitous, the way he sprawled there, and sought out her glance sympathetically with his own, seemed at first to Pippa provoking and challenging, insolently flirtatious; he had the local accent, slow and suggestive even when there was nothing to suggest. For a moment she thought he might be one of those town-boys she'd remembered from her past, but of course he was much too young for that. Twenty years younger than she was probably, or twenty-five: more like the age of her oldest son—although he wasn't looking after himself the way Toby did. Sean was muscled, but not from the gym, and there was a defiant, leering gap in his grin where one of his front teeth was missing.

She repeated to him the familiar litany of their news: that their mother was mostly sleeping, when she did wake she seemed very confused, her sisters were with her in the hospital, they were taking it in turns, the doctors couldn't predict what kind of recovery she might make, they thought the fall might have been a seizure. Sean asked if there was anything he could do, Pippa said she didn't think so, but it was very nice of him.

—I'm used to doing a few odd jobs around the place for Evelyn.

—Oh, I see, you mean for money.

He stood up on both feet away from the porch-post, frowning as if he were offended, and said he was happy to work for nothing at a time like this. Pippa felt compromised, caught out in an ungenerous assumption. —No, I'm happy to pay, but I don't think there's anything. Though I suppose there is the strimmer . . .

SO IT WAS THAT WHEN GILLIAN AND SERENA ARRIVED HOME a couple of hours later—no change at the hospital—they found the deep peace of Fern Lodge ravaged by the intrusion of the strimmer's insane snarling and whining, as Sean, shirt-less, went at the long grass in the garden, filling the air with whirling, glinting dust and shards. It had taken some com-radely effort between him and Pippa to assemble the strimmer and go through the instructions; then, while it was charg-ing, she'd made him coffee. Before he attacked the grass he'd hacked away, with a pruning knife he'd fetched from the shed as if he knew his way around, at the brambles overgrowing the flower bed.

Serena heard the strimmer as soon as she came in at the front door, took in its implications like a blow. She walked straight through the house and burst out again at the back, through the French windows in the dining room, into a scene of devastation: grass lay in heaps where it had fallen on the ragged pale stubble. White-faced, eye make-up incongruously gothic-black in the strong light, she turned on Pippa in impo-tent fury. —What have you done? she shouted. —Why did you spoil our garden? It was the only beautiful thing left here, and you've spoiled it.

Sean stopped the strimmer respectfully, seeing her ex-pression.

—It needed tidying, Pippa weakly said.

Now, when it was too late, she seemed to see how graceful the grass had been as the accompaniment to Serena's dance that morning, how it had moved with her movement. And she saw, too, how the cutting of the grass might appear as a deliberate affront, a contemptuous stroke of brute practicality against imagination and spirit. Serena had a way of construing the most harmlessly neutral acts as provocations. —We couldn't just leave it, Pippa tried to explain.

—But why not?

Her question couldn't be answered without involving all the ways the two sisters had lived their lives so differently. Sean looked tentatively between them. —Should I stop there?

Turning on him, scorning his tan and his torso, Serena hardly took him in, she was so involved in her rage against Pippa. —You might as well finish it now! The place is ruined anyway.

She stormed off; Gillian and Pippa, left behind in the familiar aftershock of one of her scenes, made wry faces at each other. Pippa said mildly to Sean that he should go ahead and cut the rest, it was all her fault, not his. Upstairs, clenching her fists, Serena stood confronting the full-length mirror in her room—her ferocity hadn't subsided, even against herself. She couldn't bear the resumption of the strimmer's noise, and thought that she had to go out; she painted her mouth with a fresh slash of lipstick, changed her heels for higher ones, fluffed up her rust-black hair, put on dark glasses; the picture-panels in the porch door juddered when she slammed it behind her. On her way down through the sloping, sleeping residential streets to the town's centre, breaking their silence with the scrape and rap of her heels, she felt at least the relief of escape—anything was better than that hospital. Then she sat solitary at an outdoor table at a café on the main street with a black coffee, long legs crossed, absorbed in lighting her cigarette and smoking it, the cigarette's poison a bravado in the face of sickness and death.

Since she'd first had any clear idea of who she was, as a teenager, Serena had seen herself set apart like this: distinguished and intriguing, dangerous, dressed in black, belonging somewhere else—outlined against the summer pastels of sloppy holidaymakers in their flip-flops, or the dowdy decency of her own family. To her credit, she'd never been interested in worldly success, or being famous—although she had been talented, in a minor way, as a singer and an actress. It had been quite hard enough work, she considered, simply becoming herself. She earned a living now working freelance as a legal secretary, cared nothing for the job and was more than competent, easily making herself indispensable. Today, in any case, over her coffee cup—intense, absent, indifferent to the place, not checking her phone, nor reading anything—she had an aura that was just as significant as if she were some celebrity, washed up improbably at the seaside, having shaken off her entourage of admirers or detractors, thirsting to be left alone with her luxuriant inward life.

The café was quiet, the town's morning bustle had subsided, its wash of holidaymakers receded. Shops were closing already, the trees' long shadows stretched at intervals across the road. On the beach, the estuary waters ran up across the flat sands, flooding the stale pools left behind that morning in cracks in the flat, layered shelves of shale; families retreated to a last redoubt, a bank of pebbles marked with a crusty high-tide line of dried seaweed, cracked plastic bottles, washed-white bones, driftwood and faded crisp packets. The water was rich with silt, chocolate brown; a few children investigated at its edge doubtfully with buckets, paddling where it foamed lazily, curling warm around their ankles, sucking underneath their soles.

SEAN MIGHT, AFTER SERENA'S PERFORMANCE IN THE GARDEN, have avoided her when he spotted her. He was making his way home, having finished strimming, to the caravan where he was living temporarily, because his wife had kicked him out; on foot because his vehicle was with his brother-in-law, who was looking at the fuel pump. But he was intrigued, and drawn to Serena dressed exotically all in black, sitting so concentrated and self-possessed with her small heart-shaped face and painted eyes and the cobwebby mass of her dark hair, not seeing him. He thought he recognised in her—in her bearing and black dress and cigarette, and the sharp point of experience in her expression—the signs of that freemasonry of difference, an alternative lifestyle, to which he also belonged in his own way, though he'd left off his earring a while ago, finding it childish.

When he was younger, there'd been a passionate frisson between boys like him and certain middle-class girls; those girls had woken up to sex when the boys of their own sort were still playing Monopoly or practising wheelies on their BMX bikes. Later the girls left, to go to university or to work elsewhere, and Sean had left too, he'd travelled around in Europe and the Far East and Australia, and then he'd come home, and got married and had two kids. Serena didn't look too bad, although he had calculated, from things her mother said, that she must be fifty at least. Her cheekbones jutted like knuckles under the white skin. But then he was no oil painting himself these days.

He stood beside the café table, said that he was sorry she was upset, waited so that she was forced to acknowledge him: she looked up as if she too felt the nudge of the old free-masonry, only wearily. —Don't worry about it. My sisters annoy me.

—You're like your mother.

She stiffened: how dare he know anything about her? —What do you mean? I'm not.

—I offered to cut the grass a couple of weeks ago and she said, No, why bother? I think she liked it the way it was, same as you.

Serena stubbed out her cigarette thoughtfully, gratified. —So then what did you do, when she said not to cut the grass? Just go away? I suppose you needed the money.

You had to be careful with the truth when it came to money, Sean knew—although he'd never for one moment have cheated the old lady. He told Serena that he'd done all sorts of odd jobs for her mother around the house: unblocking sinks and changing light bulbs, opening a jammed window, fixing the TV. In fact, though, Evelyn often couldn't think of anything for him to do; if he just sat drinking tea and talking with her, she insisted on paying him anyway. Sliding between his fingers in his pocket the two twenties Pippa had given him, he asked Serena if he could buy her another coffee; when she shook her head he believed at first that he was dismissed. —Just a glass of water, she added, glancing at passers-by in the street as if they were more interesting than he was.

It was a shame about the tooth, she thought, watching him manoeuvre competently around the tables on his way back from inside the café, bearing his own coffee and her glass; drawing up a chair opposite to hers, he sat ripping open little packets of sugar one after another to stir into his cup, which perhaps helped to explain why the tooth was missing. Still, he was good-looking: strong, brown from his work out-doors, wiry shoulder-length hair burned yellow by the sun and pushed behind his ears, a skewed long nose that might have been broken once, the hazily intent gaze of a weed-smoker. A crowned tooth would be expensive, for a casual labourer: though he told her he was trained as a joiner, with a job coming up soon at the new power station. Serena said that she hated the power station, was totally opposed to nuclear. Sean shrugged. —We need the work round here.

—You could go somewhere else.

—I tried that. Anyway, my kids are here. They stay with me at the weekends.

She smiled at him warmly, conventionally. —And how old are they?

Once his children were out in the open, they could be friendlier; Serena felt the old tide of flirtation rising between them, promising to lift her from where she was stranded. He had a girl, five, and a boy, three. —I never wanted children, she explained. —Probably because I was born with a hole in my heart: my father prayed all night to God to save me, over my crib in the hospital. I can't remember this touching scene, needless to say, but I've carried it with me, such a deadweight, all that burden of hope. After his prayers worked, he thought he owned me. It's why I've got this horrible name too.

—It's not so horrible.

—Worse than you think. Actually I'm Angel: Angel Serena. You can imagine why I dropped the Angel part. Mum had nothing to do with choosing it, Dad was the sentimental one. Did you know he was headmaster at Daresbrook? He was an awful bully. I'm glad he was never my headmaster.

Sean had gone to Daresbrook, but it must have been after her father retired.

—We heard that it went to the dogs, she said. —But then he would say that, wouldn't he?

He tried to weigh his experience at school impartially. —I wasn't the right type, he confessed, rueful. —Didn't react well to being confined in a classroom.

—You were probably one of the dogs. I mean, that my father thought it went to.

Wondering whether to feel insulted, Sean said that he regretted it now. —I wish I had my time over again.

She widened her eyes at him, doubting it, and said she never regretted anything. Whatever happened, had to be that way. As she spoke, however, she was waylaid by a vision of her mother in that hospital bed, so shrunken, her skin yellowed and jaw slack, absent from herself, held up between the bleeping heart monitor and drip and catheter, the tight old knot of her long life loosening, coming undone. The sadness that had evaded Serena when she'd searched for it, so that she'd believed her own heart was a dry husk, found her here in the café when she least expected it. She blotted her eyes with a tissue, sipped from her glass of water.

—It's a difficult time for you, Sean sympathetically said.

He covered her small cool hand on the table with his own, which was huge and hot, calloused across the top of the palm, black dirt rimmed round the nails. Of course Serena couldn't begin to describe all of her private difficulty, not to a stranger. She pulled her hand away and spoke instead about climate change, the political chaos that must follow it, the world running away from them, despair of the future. —I should do something, she said, —I know that I should act. But I don't have any conviction. I'm no good at conviction.

Sean wrote his phone number on the back of his receipt from the café. —Text me, he said, —so that I've got your number too.

—All right, I will.

—No, do it now.

She smiled, watery-eyed, at his scrap of paper lying untouched on the table between them.

—Go on, you might as well. In case you need anything, any odd jobs doing.

She wouldn't text him while he watched. But she picked up his number before she went, dropped it into her bag.

THAT EVENING WHILE PIPPA AND GILLIAN WATCHED TELEVI-sion, Serena went rummaging through the cupboards upstairs, renewed and energised. Her sisters were still jarred by the scene she'd made; she'd always had this trick, of unleashing her worst and then being the first to recover from it. —Look what I've found! she sang out, but the others were reluctant to move from in front of their documentary on Minoan Crete. —Come and see! It's the Bunty Club.

—Oh, the Bunty Club!

Gillian was perplexed. —The what?

—You remember the Bunty Club! We had secret club meetings in the shed. *We swear not to do good, and never to help people.*

—I've got no memory of it. Were we horrid?

—It was just a reaction to Daddy, Pippa reassured her. —The actual bad things we did were terribly innocent, mostly. I think we hid his slippers, dug up some potatoes he'd planted in the garden. He always thought it was a fox. We jammed Mum's knitting machine. *Bunty* was the comic we wanted, and he said it wasn't suitable, we were only allowed *Look and Learn.*

—It's a treasure trove, Serena said. She stood blocking their view of the television, with a cardboard box in her arms, reading aloud from papers inside it. —*Chairman Philippa Anne Styles drew the meeting to a close with three cheers for Bunty Club members for all their hard work on doing wrong. Vice Chairman Gillian Elizabeth Styles seconded the motion.* Who knew you were such budding bureaucrats? And actually wasn't it usually me doing the wrong, under orders from you two?

—You enjoyed it, Pippa briskly said. —You wanted to be in the club. And we knew you wouldn't get in as much trouble as us if you were caught, because you were little and they always said you didn't know what you were doing, though I'm sure you knew perfectly well.

Serena dumped the box on the carpet; her sisters knelt heavily beside her to unpack it, exclaiming over the contents. There were minutes of club meetings and lists of enemies and bad deeds, a top-secret code-book, home-made badges covered in Fablon which fastened with safety pins on the back, a dried-up ink pad, a date stamp turned to the fifth of October 1969. *Miss A. S. Styles was permitted to enter the meeting on strict condition of sharing all sweets and other grub etc.* All the paperwork was typed, the individual letters not quite aligned and indented deep into the paper, wavering between black ink and red; they had acquired a typewriter when the parish office bought a new one, and it had seemed biblical in itself, presiding over their playroom, as ancient as Methuselah, too heavy for them to lift, its action thunderous and punitive. When a locked tin cash box rattled intriguingly, Pippa levered it open with a screwdriver from the understairs cupboard, and after a moment's perplexity remembered that its contents were the club's Sacred Objects: a bone, a crumpled page from a prayer book (—We spat on it, she said), a wrapped razor blade, their father's bronze medal for swimming, a gold ring set flashily with a green stone.

—A stolen ring, Pippa announced, suddenly quite certain.
—We actually stole it.

—No! Who from?

—No idea. I knew once, but now I'm simply blank. Not from our parents, obviously—anyway, it isn't their taste. Imagine Mummy wearing this! The name of the victim ought to haunt us, oughtn't it? So much for a bad conscience.

—We could have it valued.

Pippa dropped the ring back into the cash box. —Best not, perhaps.

The textures of the past rose around the sisters like an uneasy dream, alien and stale and intensely familiar. For twenty minutes it was intoxicating, hilarious. Then, in the present, they began to be bored and their knees were stiff. Gillian still insisted that she couldn't remember the club. She was distracted by the television; she and Pippa had visited the palace at Knossos a few years ago with their husbands, who didn't get on; Pippa had sprained her ankle clambering on the ruins. That was an awful holiday.

GILLIAN HAD GIVEN HER MOBILE NUMBER TO THE HOSPITAL ward. She left the phone charging on her bedside table, and was woken very early the next morning by its ringing; whatever her dreams had been, they dispersed in that instant, iridescence breaking up on the surface of deep water. Abruptly she sat up in bed, pressed the green circle without fumbling. The same nurse who'd been on duty the day before said in an emotional voice that the sisters should come into the hospital at once. They would leave as soon as they were dressed, Gillian said. Leaping up, sick with excitement and dread, she crossed to the window and parted the curtains, looking out into the garden's subdued blue light as if she had to check it was still there: massy forms of the apple trees, black incontrovertible bulk of the shed, birds stirring invisible in the undergrowth. This was the exceptional, the awaited day. She was seized and rigid in its tension; she knew she must go to her sisters at once and wake them, tell them to get ready, yet she had its revelation for this one moment to herself. Alone, she rose to the occasion. Through the open window came the cool long breath of earth.

Then, finally, she remembered the Bunty Club—not all the funny detail but the actuality of it, the clandestine meetings in the shed, crouching on the floor amongst all those dangerous tools they weren't supposed to go near, the splintery plank walls fragrant with creosote, her arms wrapped tight around scabbed knees, feeling scalded and enthralled by what was forbidden. The shed was ripe with the smells of tomato plants, 3-in-One oil, mealworms for the bird table, crusts of cut grass souring on the blades of the mower; beams of brilliant light from knotholes pierced its stuffy dimness. Her thighs were wet with sweat under her shorts and her silky hair, cut off at shoulder length, tickled her freckled arms, which tasted sun-baked as she sucked at her own skin, leaving purple marks. Clever Pippa had got the idea for their club out of the storybooks whose contents she seemed to absorb so effortlessly, and with actual pleasure. Before Pippa grew into a teenager, and lost her nerve, she had been so full of ideas; running in the garden and in races on Sports Day with such flat-footed eager assurance, plait flicking bossily behind her, plain long face raised to the sun. Gillian had adored and envied her, felt herself formless and dull by contrast.

The house was still quiet, her sisters hadn't been woken by the phone ringing. Important with her mission, she went out onto the landing, calling their names in a low voice, raising her hand to knock before she poked her head around their bedroom doors into the fusty half-light. She had the odd sensation of resuming some ceremonial left unfinished a long time ago; then she remembered how fervently she and Pippa had prayed, after Serena was born, for her to live. Their actual baby sister, when eventually she came home from hospital, had been problematic and prosaic, if more or less lovable, and not the all-transforming mystery they'd thirsted for. Was this the mystery now? Gillian tried to imagine their mother calling them in from the garden for tea, standing in her apron in the kitchen doorway—but the indefinite figure wouldn't come into focus, dissolving like her dream. In their bedrooms her sisters were rousing from sleep, lifting their heads to stare at her, confused, wrapped embryonic in the cocoons of their duvets, not ready yet for her news.

My Mother's Wedding

IT WAS NEVER GOING TO BE THE ORDINARY KIND OF WEDDING. My mother didn't do anything ordinary. She would marry Patrick at the summer solstice; it would all take place on the smallholding where we lived, in Pembrokeshire. My parents had bought the place in the seventies from an old couple, Welsh-speaking and chapel-going. Family and friends were coming from all over, all our Pembrokeshire friends would be there, and those of our neighbours who were still our friends—some of them didn't like the way we lived. My mother had dreamed up a wedding ceremony with plenty of drama. She and Patrick would drink Fen's home-made mead from a special cup, then smash it; the clinching moment would come when they got to take off all their clothes at sunset and immerse themselves in the pond while everyone sang. Then Fen would wave myrtle branches over them and pronounce them man and wife. Mum had spent hours puzzling in her notebook, trying to devise the right form of words for her vow. She could whisper to horses (she really could, that wasn't just hokum, I've seen her quieting a berserk half-broken young colt when grown men wouldn't go near it), but she struggled sometimes to find the right words for things.

Patrick wasn't my father, needless to say. My father was long gone: from the smallholding and from West Wales and from the lifestyle. Dad had short hair now, he worked for an insurance company and voted for Mrs. Thatcher. From time to time I went to stay with him and my stepmother, and I thought of those weeks in High Barnet as a tranquil escape, the way other people enjoyed a holiday in the country: with their central heating, and their kitchen with its food processor and waste-disposal unit, and the long empty days while they were both out at work, when I tried on all her trim little dresses and her make-up. I never mentioned Mrs. Thatcher when I got back to Wales. I didn't like her politics any more than the others did, but I loved my dad. I didn't want to encourage the way everyone gloated, pretending to be shocked and disappointed by how he'd gone over to the dark side.

Patrick wasn't the father of my two half-siblings, Eithne and Rowan, either. Their dad was Lawrence, and he was still very much in our lives, lived a mile down the road—only he'd left Mum around the time Rowan was starting school, went off with Nancy Withers. And on the rebound Mum had had a fling with Fen, who was her best friend Sue's husband. But that was all over now and Patrick was the love of her life and someone new from outside our set. All those people from her past—Lawrence and Nancy and Fen and Sue and all the others, though not my dad or my stepmother—would be at her wedding because that was the sort of party they all liked best, where everyone had a history with everyone else, and anything might happen, and there was opportunity for plenty of pouring out their hearts to one another and dancing and pairing up in the wrong pairs—while the dope and the drink and the mushroom-brew kept everything lubricated and crazy. Meanwhile, the ragged gang of their kids would be running wild around the place in the dark, much wilder than their parents knew, stealing Fen's disgusting mead and spying on what they never should have seen—and one of them would almost inevitably break an arm, or set fire to a tent, or nearly drown. (Once, at a different party, one of the children really did drown, but that's another story.)

And I wouldn't know what to do with myself, because at seventeen I was too old to run with the kids, yet I was still holding back—too wary and angry and sceptical—from joining in with the adults. I was pretty much angry about everything, around that time. My mother came draping herself over my shoulders where I was trying to learn about photo-synthesis out of the textbook for my Biology A level. —Janey, precious-heart, help me with this wretched vow-thing, I can't get it right. You're the one who's clever with words. What should I say? I've put *I promise to worship the loving man in you,* but then I have this picture of Patrick flinging it back at me if ever anything went wrong. Because of course I know what can happen, I know about men, I'm not going into this with my eyes closed.

—Mum, get off, I said, trying to ease myself out from under her, —I can't possibly make up your wedding vows. It's inappropriate.

—You're such an old stick-in-the-mud, she said fondly, squeezing my shoulders tightly and kissing the top of my head, her auburn hair flopping down onto the page. Her hair is like Elizabeth Siddal's in Rossetti's paintings and she wears it either loose or in a rope wrapped around her head, and actually her looks are like Elizabeth Siddal's too, and she wears the same drapey clothes. But I was the one who knew who Elizabeth Siddal was, and that Rossetti buried her with a book of his poems and then dug her up again to get them back; I knew all about the Pre-Raphaelites and Rossetti and Burne-Jones and the rest, and I didn't even like them all that much. That was the way life was divided up between me and my mother. I knew about things, and she was beautiful.

I couldn't imagine Patrick flinging anything back at anyone. Patrick had the sweetest temperament. He was much younger than Mum, only twenty-six, closer to my age than hers, and he was loose-limbed with messy pale hair, and sleepy grey eyes as though everything in his life had been a dream until he woke up and saw my mother—in the wholefood cooperative in the village, as it happened, when they both reached for a paper sack of muesli base at the same moment. He'd come out to West Wales to stay in a friend's family's holiday home for a couple of months, to finish his PhD thesis on the theology of Julian of Norwich (I knew who she was too). He'd run out of grant money and told us he'd been living for weeks on nothing much but apples and muesli base. —It's very filling, he said cheerfully. Mum thought he was other-worldly like the Celtic saints, but I knew he was just an intellectual. He'd never properly come up against life in its full force before: he fell for the first real thing he laid his eyes on, like an innocent in a Shakespeare play. There was a girlfriend back in Oxford—another theologian—but she didn't have a chance against that rope of auburn hair. He'd abandoned the thesis too.

We loved Patrick, Eithne and Rowan and me. Eithne and Rowan loved rambling with him around our land, showing him everything, amazed because he hadn't done any of the things they took for granted: had never swung out on a rope over the river, or ridden a pony bareback (or ridden any way at all), had never seen anything like the dead crows strung up along the fence wire of the neighbouring farmer who hated us. I loved talking with someone who had read things in books, instead of having experiences. Experience was etched into the tanned, leathery faces of all the other adults in my life; their experience—and that meant sex, mostly—was a calculating light in their eyes when they looked at me. Patrick and I sank deep in the sagging old sofa which stank of the dogs, while my mother cooked vats of curry for the freezer, and he told me about Julian of Norwich, and I was happy. This doesn't mean I was keen on his marrying my mother.

I KEPT SAYING IT WOULD RAIN ON THE WEDDING PARTY because it's always raining in Wales (that's another nice thing about High Barnet). —We ought to make plans for the rain, I said, but my mother just smiled and said she knew it was going to be fine, and then it was: the day dawned cloudless and pure, yellow haze gleaming in the meadows, hills in the distance delicately drawn in blue. I had to hold on very firmly, sometimes, to my conviction that everything could be explained in the light of reason; it really did seem as though Mum had witch-powers. She could smell if rain was coming, her dreams seemed to foretell the future, and her hands could feel for the place where a horse was hurt, or a child. People said her touch was healing—only I didn't want her touching me, not any more.

She and I worked together all that morning, defrosting the curries and loaves of wholemeal bread and the dishes of crumble we'd cooked with our own apples and quinces, mixing jugs of home-made lemonade. Fen drove over with plastic buckets of mead and crates of bottles in the back of his flatbed, along with a suspect carrier bag: he was in charge of the stronger stuff. Sue had sent the wedding cake, soaked in brandy and decorated with hearts and flowers cut out in coloured marzipan. —You don't think it's poisoned? I said. —After what you did to her? My mother only laughed. —We've forgiven each other everything. Anyway, Sue started it—when she slept with your dad, while I was still breast-feeding you.

I pretended I knew about this, just to prevent her telling me any more. Then I sorted out sleeping bags and blankets for all the guests who were going to stay over. Patrick helped me haul the old mattresses up into the hayloft in our barn, built of ancient grey stone, older and more spacious than the farmhouse. When we stood at the open loft window with the sweet air blowing around us—it was tall as the loft itself, gracious as a church window, only without any glass—we could see ten miles, all the way to the glinting fine line of the sea.

—Are you sure you want to go through with this? I said daringly. —I know Mum's very overwhelming.

I expected him to reply with the same dazed absent-mindedness I was used to, as if he were under her spell—and was surprised when he looked at me sharply. —I suppose you think she's too old for me, he said.

I made some joke about cradle-snatching.

—She looks great though, doesn't she? Patrick went on uneasily. —For her age.

So he wasn't so other-worldly after all! I didn't know whether to be triumphant, or disappointed in him.

OUR GUESTS BEGAN TO ARRIVE IN THE AFTERNOON. THE PARTY grew around the outdoor fireplace Lawrence had built in the meadow years ago, when he still lived with us. Lawrence was handsome, big and ruddy-faced with thick black hair and side-burns and moustache; he made his living as a builder though he'd been to one of the famous public schools. He was in charge of barbecuing as usual, and we brought out all the rest of the food too, from the kitchen, to keep warm beside his fire. Fen—not handsome in the least but wickedly funny, tall and stooped with a shaved head and huge crooked nose—started doling out the drink. I wouldn't drink, and they all thought it was because I was a puritan, controlled and disapproving; actually the reason was rather different. A year ago, at another party, when no one was looking I'd helped myself to too much mushroom-liquor from the bottom of one of Fen's brews, and since then I'd been accompanied everywhere by a minor hallucination, hearing my own feet tapping on the floor like little trotting hooves. Nothing disastrous, but enough to scare me.

Patrick had scythed along the top of the meadow that morning and smells of fresh-cut grass and roasting meat mingled together. Swallows came darting and mewing among the clouds of insects in the slanting yellow light. When the Irish band turned up, Mum and Patrick danced the first dance alone, then everyone else joined in; the warmth seemed to thicken as the sun sank lower. The kids had found our old punt in the long grass and taken it out on the pond; it leaked and they had to bail it frantically. The sounds of their distant shouting and laughter and splashing, and the dogs barking at them, all came scudding back to us across the water. I thought that my sister Eithne must be down at the pond with the others, until I caught sight of her at the heart of the dancing—and she looked as if she'd been drinking too. There was always trouble at our parties (my little hooves didn't begin to count, in the scale of things), and this time the trouble began with Eithne.

She was fourteen, and her face was expressive enough when she was sober, with her big loose mouth and bright auburn hair, and the funny cast in one of her hazel eyes like a black inkblot; she was wearing her pale old stretch-towelling pyjamas to dance in, and had her hair done in several plaits that bounced around her head like snakes. Eithne had all sorts of mystery illnesses; I used to get mad because I thought Mum kept her home from school on the least excuse, or if she just thought the teacher wasn't being spiritual enough. So Eithne could hardly read or write, she didn't know basic things like fractions or the date of the French Revolution—probably didn't know the French Revolution had even happened. But she'd always been able to dance like a dream, the same graceful easy way that she could ride and swim.

While Mum and Patrick were drinking out of the wedding cup, which Nancy Withers had made specially, Eithne came snuggling up next to me. I felt the waves of drunkenness go shuddering through her skinny body. —Have you been at Fen's mead? I asked her. —You'll make yourself sick.

—I don't care if I die, she said.

—You won't die. You'll just be throwing up all night.

Mum promised to love the holy wanderer in Patrick, and Patrick promised, because he could quote poetry, to love the pilgrim soul in Mum. They lifted the wedding cup between them and smashed it down against the stones of Lawrence's fireplace, then kissed passionately. Eithne said it was disgusting, and that she was going to bed.

—I told you you'd make yourself sick, I said.

Then when she'd gone, Mum and Patrick were smooching together for a while to the sound of the band, until Mum suddenly had one of her intuitions. She pushed Patrick away and went running up towards the house with her skirts pulled up around her knees so she could go faster. And somehow I must have half-shared in the intuition because I went running up after her, and as we left the meadow behind and came round the side of the farmhouse we could see Eithne standing framed against the last of the light, in her pyjamas, in the barn's hayloft window—which wasn't really a window at all, just an opening into the air, fifteen feet above the ground.

—Ethie, take care! Mum called out. —Step back from the window, my darling.

—I love Patrick, Eithne said. —I don't want you to marry him.

And then she stepped forward out of the window into nothingness, flopping down like a doll and landing with a thud on a heap of rubble overgrown with nettles. Mum ran forward with an awful cry and picked her up out of the nettles, and I really thought my sister must be dead—but by some miracle she wasn't hurt, apart from the nettle stings. (Mum said afterwards it was because she'd fallen with her limbs so floppy and relaxed.) Cradling Eithne in her arms, she told me to go and tell Patrick to wait for her. —I've got to deal with this, she said. And she carried Eithne into the house and lay on the bed upstairs with her, soothing her, making everything all right. This is the sort of thing that happens at our parties.

EVERYONE INCLUDING THE BAND HAD DRIFTED DOWN THE meadow to stand beside the pond. The kids had pulled the punt out into the grass and now everyone was waiting for the finale, when Mum and Patrick took off their clothes and walked into the water. Patrick stood at the edge by himself with his clothes still on, looking doubtful. The sun was going down behind the row of beech trees that marked the edge of our smallholding, and its light made a shining path across the water's surface, motionless as glass. I don't know what made me do the mad thing I did next; perhaps it was the last kick of my year-long mushroom-hallucination. Instead of giving Mum's message to Patrick, I put my arms around his neck and kissed him. —Mum's not coming, I said. —Marry me.

—Janey says Patrick ought to marry her instead, Fen announced to everyone, booming, waving his myrtle branch.

—Marry me, I said, louder.

—Where is she, anyway? Patrick looked around him helplessly.

—Marry her, marry Janey instead, they all called encouragingly, maliciously: Lawrence and Fen, Nancy and Sue, and all the rest.

The fiddle player started up the Wedding March.

And I pulled my dress over my head and stepped out of my knickers and unhooked my bra, not looking at anyone though I knew they were all looking at me, and I waded naked into the pond water along the shining path, up to my knees and then up to my thighs, feeling the silt oozing between my toes, not caring about the sinister, slippery things that touched me. It was such a risk, it would have been so humiliating if Patrick hadn't come in after me. I waited, not looking back at him, looking ahead at the sunset glowing like a fire between the beeches, while he stood hesitating on the brink. I heard them all singing and I felt the first drops of rain on my skin, like a sign.

Funny Little Snake

THE CHILD WAS NINE YEARS OLD AND COULDN'T FASTEN HER own buttons. Valerie knelt in front of her on the carpet in the spare room and Robyn held out first one cuff and then the other without a word, then turned around to present the back of her dress, where a long row of spherical chocolate-brown buttons was unfastened over a grubby white petticoat edged with lace. The skinny tiny shoulder blades flickered with repressed movement. And although every night since Robyn had arrived, a week ago, Valerie had encouraged her into a bath foamed up with bubbles, she still smelled of something furtive—musty spice from the back of a cupboard. The smell must be in her dress, which Valerie didn't dare wash because it looked as though it had to be dry-cleaned, or in her skin, or in her lank liquorice-coloured hair, which was pushed back from her forehead under an even grubbier stretch Alice band. Trust Robyn's mother to have a child who couldn't do up buttons, and then put her in a fancy plaid dress with hundreds of them, and frogging and leg-of-mutton sleeves, like a Victorian orphan, instead of ordinary slacks and a T-shirt so that she could play. The mother went around, apparently, in long dresses and bare feet, and had her picture painted by artists. Robyn at least had come wearing tights, and plimsoll shoes with elastic tops—though her green coat was too thin for winter weather.

Valerie had tried to talk to her stepdaughter. It was the first time they'd met, and she'd braced herself for resentment, the child's mind poisoned against her. Robyn was miniature, a doll—with a plain, pale, wide face, her temples blue-veined where her hair was strained back, her wide-open grey eyes affronted and evasive and set too far apart. She wasn't naughty, and she wasn't actually silent—that would have been a form of stubbornness to combat, to coax and manoeuvre round. She was a nullity, an absence, answering yes and no obediently if she was questioned, in that languid drawl that was some-how so offensive—though Valerie knew the accent wasn't the child's fault, only what she'd learned. Robyn even said please and thank you, and she told Valerie the name of her teacher, but when Valerie asked whether she liked the teacher—she hadn't liked her own teachers much, when she was at school—her look slipped away uneasily from her stepmother's and she shrugged, as if such an idea as liking or not liking hadn't occurred to her. The only dislikes she was definite about had to do with eating. When Valerie put fish pie on Robyn's plate on the first night, she shot her a direct look of such pierc-ing desperation—she hardly ever actually appealed, or asked for anything—that Valerie, who was a good wholesome cook and had been going to insist, asked her kindly what she ate at home. Eggs? Cottage pie? Baked beans?

Honestly, the girl hardly seemed to know the names of things. Toast, was all she could think of. Definitely not eggs: a vehement head-shake. Toast, and—after long consideration, then murmuring hesitantly, tonelessly—tomato soup, corn-flakes, butterscotch Instant Whip. It was lucky that Gil wasn't witness to these negotiations over food, because he would have thought Valerie was spoiling his daughter. He and Val-erie ate together later, after Robyn was in bed. Gil might be a left-winger in his politics—Harold Wilson had rung him up once to ask him about strategy with the trade unions, he often dropped that into conversation—but he was old-fashioned in his values at home. He despised, for instance, the little box of a house the university had given them, and wanted to move into one of the rambling old mansions on the road behind his office; he thought they had more style, with their peeling paint and big gardens overgrown with trees.

Valerie didn't tell him how much she enjoyed all the con-veniences of their modern home—the clean light rooms, the central heating, the electric tin-opener fitted on the kitchen wall. And she was intrigued, because Gil was old-fashioned, by his having chosen for his first wife a woman who went barefoot and lived like a hippie in her big Chelsea flat. Perhaps Marise had been so beautiful once, that Gil couldn't resist her: Valerie was twenty-four, she didn't think Marise could still be beautiful at forty. Now, anyway, he called her the Rat-trap, and the Beak, and the Bitch-from-hell, and said she would fuck anyone. When Valerie first married him, she hadn't believed that a professor could know such words. She'd known them herself, of course, but that was different, she wasn't educated.

On the phone to his ex-wife, Gil had made a lot of fuss about having his daughter to visit, as a stubborn point of pride, and then had driven all the way down in the Morris Traveller to London to fetch her. But since they got back he'd gone out every day, although it wasn't term-time, to work on the book he was writing in his office at the university, saying he needed absolute concentration. Robyn didn't seem to miss him. She looked bemused when Valerie called him her daddy, as if she hardly recognised him by that name; she'd only been three or four when he moved out from living with Marise. If Gil came in from work while Robyn was watching the television, she slipped down from the sofa and stood with her flat, absorbent little face presented to him like an empty slate waiting for a mark. —Splendid, he only said, patting at her with awkward vagueness. —So you two are getting on. Valerie can't resist her goggle-box: I see you're both as bad as each other!

Valerie didn't ask Gil what he'd talked about with his daughter on the long car journey: perhaps they'd driven the whole way in silence. Or perhaps he'd questioned Robyn about her mother, or ranted on about her, or talked about his work. Sometimes in the evenings he talked to Valerie for hours about university politics or other historians he envied or resented—or even about the Civil War or the Long Parliament or the idea of the state—without noticing that she wasn't listening, she was thinking about new curtains or counting the stitches in her knitting. He might have found fatherhood easier, Valerie thought, if Robyn had been pretty. Moodily, after Robyn had gone to bed, Gil wondered aloud whether she was really even his. —Who knows, with the Great Whore of Marylebone putting it about like there's no tomorrow? The child's half-feral, she doesn't look anything like me. Is she normal? Do they even send her to school? I think she's backward. A little bit simple, stunted. No surprises, growing up in that sink of iniquity. God only knows what she's seen.

Valerie was getting to know the way that he used exaggerated expressions like *sink of iniquity,* whose sense she didn't recognise but could guess at, as if he were partly mocking his own disapproval, while at the same time he furiously meant it. He kept one step ahead of any fixed position, so that no one could catch him out in it. But Robyn looked more like him than he realised, although she was smooth and bland with childhood and he was hoary and sagging from fifty years' experience. He had the same pale skin as hers, and the same startled hare's eyes, swimming in and out of focus behind his big black-framed glasses. Sometimes when Gil laughed you could see how he might have been a different man if he hadn't chosen to be this professor with his stooping bulk and crumpled shapeless suits, his braying, brilliant talk. Without glasses, his face was naked and keen and boyish, with a boy's shame, as if the nakedness must be smothered like a secret, under layers of disavowal.

Gil's widowed mother had owned a small newsagent's, he'd got himself to university and then onwards through his achievements into success and even fame—he'd been on television often—through his own sheer cleverness and effort. Not that he tried to hide his class origins: on the contrary, he'd honed them into a weapon to use against his colleagues and friends, deriding them for their privilege. But he always repeated the same few anecdotes from his childhood, worn smooth from use: the brewhouse in the backyard where the women gossiped and did their washing, the bread-and-dripping suppers, a neighbour cutting his throat in the shared toilet, his mother polishing the front step with Cardinal Red. He didn't talk about his mother in private, and when Valerie once asked him how she died he wouldn't tell her anything except—gruffly barking it, as if to frighten her off and mock her fear at the same time—that it was cancer. She guessed that he'd probably been close to his mother, and then grown up to be embarrassed by her, and hated himself for neglecting her, but couldn't admit to any of this because he was always announcing publicly how much he loathed sentimentality and guilt. Valerie had been attracted to him in the first place because he made fun of everything, nothing was sacred. She was the same way herself.

She didn't really want the child around. But it was only fair, and she had always bargained with the existence of Robyn as part of what she paid for having been singled out by the professor among the girls in the faculty office in King's College London, marrying him, moving with him to begin their new life in the North—there had been some quarrel or other with King's, he had enemies there. As the week wore on, though, she grew sick of the sound of her own voice jollying Robyn along, acting out the nice time they weren't really having. She hadn't even brought any toys with her, to occupy her time. After a while Valerie noticed that, when no one was looking, she played with two weird little figures, scraps of cloth tied into shapes with wool, one in each hand, doing the voices almost inaudibly. One voice was coaxing and hopeful, the other one reluctant. *Put on your special gloves,* one of them said. *But I don't like blue colour,* said the other. *These ones have special powers,* the first voice persisted. *Try them out.*

Valerie asked Robyn if these were her dollies. Shocked out of her fantasy, she hid the scraps behind her back. —Not really, she said.

—What are their names?

—They don't have names.

—We could get out my sewing machine and make clothes for them.

She shook her head, alarmed. —They don't need clothes.

When Valerie tied her into an apron, and stood her on a chair to make scones, Robyn's fingers went burrowing into the flour as if they were independent of her, mashing the butter into lumps in her hot palms. —Like this, Valerie said, showing her how to lift the flour as she rubbed, for lightness. Playfully, she grabbed at Robyn's fingers under the surface of the flour, but Robyn snatched them back, and wouldn't try the scones when they were baked. Valerie ended up eating them, although she was trying to watch her weight, sticking to Ryvita and cottage cheese for lunch: she didn't want to run to fat like her mother. She thought Gil refused to visit her mother partly because he worried over how Valerie might look one day, when she wasn't soft and fresh and blonde any longer.

Robyn had hardly brought enough clothes to last the week—as well as the dress with the buttons there was only a grey skirt that looked like a school uniform, a ribbed nylon jumper, one spare pair of knickers, odd socks, and a full-length nightdress made of red wool flannel like something out of a storybook. The nightdress smelled of wee and anyway Valerie thought it must be itchy; she took Robyn shopping in town for sensible pyjamas and they had tea in the cafeteria in British Home Stores, which used to be Valerie's treat when she was Robyn's age. Robyn didn't want a meringue but asked if she was allowed to hold her new pyjamas, then sat self-consciously with the cellophane package in her lap. The pyjamas were white, decorated with yellow and blue pictures of yachts and anchors. —Can I keep them? she asked tentatively, after a long dull silence. Valerie had grown tired of chatting away inanely to no one.

She had been going to suggest Robyn leave the pyjamas behind, ready for the next time she visited, but she didn't really care. Every child ought to want something, it was only healthy. And packed into Robyn's suitcase along with the rest of her clothes—all freshly washed apart from the dress, and pressed, even the socks, with Valerie's steam iron—the pyjamas would be like a message, a coded reproach, for Robyn's mother; she imagined Marise unpacking them guiltily, in some room in Chelsea she couldn't really visualise. Valerie knew, however, that her own performance of scrupulous caring was a lie, because the truth was that she couldn't wait for Robyn to go home. She longed to be free from that dogged unresponsive little figure following her everywhere around the house, or lying limp and dumb in her lap after a bath while Valerie briskly towelled her, because she didn't know how to dry herself. Robyn went to bed dressed in the new pyjamas, clutching her scrap-figures as usual, one in either hand; they weren't any more than squares of material scrunched up and tied in the middle to make a head, eyes and smiling mouth drawn in felt pen. Selena had made them for her, she told Valerie, who worked out Selena must have been the cleaner. —She doesn't come any more, Robyn added, though not as if she minded particularly—in her most flattening clipped tones, like a real little Lady Muck. —We sacked her. She stole things.

GIL WAS SUPPOSED TO BE DRIVING ROBYN BACK DOWN TO London on the Wednesday. On the Tuesday evening when he came home early Valerie knew right away something was up. He stood behind her where she was preparing meatloaf at the kitchen counter, nuzzling under her ear and stroking her breast with one hand, jigging the ice cubes determinedly in his Scotch with the other. He always poured himself a generous Scotch as soon as he came in: she'd learned not to comment. —You're so good to me, he said pleadingly, his voice muffled in her neck. —I don't deserve it.

—Oh dear, what's Mr. Naughty's little game now? Valerie was long-suffering, faintly amused, swiping onions from her chopping board into a bowl with the side of her knife. —What's he sniffing after? He wants something.

—He knows he's so selfish. Causes her no end of trouble.

These were two of the roles they played out sometimes: Valerie brusquely competent and in charge, Gil wheedling and needy. There was some truth behind all their performances, as well as pretence. Gil groaned apologetically. Something had come up at work tomorrow, a special guest to dinner at High Table, someone he needed to meet because he had influence and the whole game was a bloody conspiracy. He'd never be able to get back in time from London. And Thursday was no good either, faculty meeting; Friday he was giving a talk in Manchester. They could keep Robyn until Saturday, but the She-Bitch would never let him hear the end of it. He wanted Valerie to take her home tomorrow on the train. Valerie could stay over with her mother in Acton, couldn't she? Come back the following day.

Valerie had counted on being free from tomorrow morning, getting the house back to normal, having her thoughts to herself again, catching a bus into town perhaps, shopping. She was gasping for her solitude like a lungful of clean air. Calculating swiftly, biting her lower lip to stop herself blurting out a protest, she kneaded onions with her hand into the minced meat cold from the fridge; the recipe came from a magazine, it was seasoned with allspice and tomato ketchup. Certainly she didn't fancy three extra days with the kid moping around. She thought with a flush of outrage how Gil was truly selfish, never taking her needs into consideration; but on the other hand the selfishness of important men was part of their dignity, they had to be selfish in order to get on with their work and get ahead, she understood that. She wouldn't have wanted a kinder, softer man who wasn't respected. And she could squeeze concessions out of him, in return for this favour. It was true that her mother was always complaining she never visited. And perhaps she'd ring up one of her old girlfriends, meet for coffee in

Oxford Street, or even for a gin in a pub for old times' sake, buy herself something new to wear. She had money saved up that Gil didn't know about, out of the housekeeping.

Theatrically she sighed. —It's very inconvenient. I was going to go into Jones's, to make enquiries about these curtains for the sitting room.

He didn't even correct her and tell her to call it the drawing room.

—He's sorry, he's really sorry. It isn't fair, he knows it. But it could be a little holiday for you. You could just put Robyn into a cab at the station, give the driver the address, let her mother pay. Why shouldn't she? She's got money.

Valerie was startled that he could even think she'd do that. The child could hardly get herself dressed in the mornings, she certainly wasn't fit to be knocking halfway around London by herself, bargaining with cab drivers. And anyway, if Valerie really was going all the way to London, she might as well have a glimpse of where her stepdaughter lived. She was afraid of Marise, but curious about her too.

OUTSIDE THE FRONT DOOR IN CHELSEA, VALERIE STOOD HOLDING Robyn's suitcase in one leather-gloved hand and her own overnight bag in the other. The house was grand and dilapidated, set back from the street in an overgrown garden, with a flight of stone steps rising to a scruffy pillared portico, a broad door painted black. Names in faded rain-stained ink were drawing-pinned beside a row of bells; they'd already rung twice and Valerie's feet were like ice; afternoon light was thickening gloomily under the evergreens. Robyn stood beside her uncomplaining in her thin coat, although from time to time on their journey Valerie had seen her quake with the cold as if it probed her, bypassing her conscious mind, like a jolt of electricity. The heating had been faulty on the train. While Valerie read her magazines and Robyn worked dutifully and unenthusiastically through one page after another in her colouring book, the washed-out numb winter landscape had borne cruelly in on them from beyond the window in their compartment: miles of bleached tufted dun grasses, purple-black tangled labyrinths of bramble, clumps of dark reeds frozen in a ditch. Valerie had been relieved when they got into the dirty old city at last. She hadn't taken to the North, though she was trying.

Staring up at the front door, Robyn had her usual stolidly neutral look, buffered against expectation; she hardly seemed excited by the prospect of seeing her mother again. And when eventually the door swung open, a young man about Valerie's age—with long fair hair and a flaunting angel face, dark-stubbled jaw, dead cigarette stuck to the wet of his sagging lip—looked out at them without any recognition. —Oh, hullo? he said.

With his peering dozy eyes he might have only just got out of bed, or be about to slop back into it at any moment, and he seemed to be bursting out of his tight clothes: a shrunken T-shirt exposed a long hollow of skinny brown belly and slick line of dark hairs, leading down inside pink satin hipster trousers. His feet were bare just as Valerie had expected, and tufted with more hair, and he smelled like a zoo animal, of something sour and choking. Recognition dawned, when he noticed Robyn. —Hullo! he said, as if it were funny. —You're the little girl.

—Is Mrs. Hope at home? Valerie asked stiffly.

He scratched his chest under the T-shirt and his smile slid back to dwell on her, making her conscious of her breasts although he'd only quickly flicked his glance across them. —Yeah, somewhere.

A woman came clattering downstairs behind him, loomed across his shoulder; she was taller than he was, statuesque, tremendous in the shadows, glittering eyes black with make-up and diamonds glinting in the piled-up mass of her dark hair, in the middle of the afternoon. Though of course the diamonds were paste, it was all a joke, a pantomime send-up, Valerie wasn't such a fool, she got that. Still, Marise was spectacular in a long low-cut white dress and white patent leather boots; she had an exaggerated coarse beauty, like a film star blurred from being too much seen. —Oh Christ, is it today? Shit! Is that the kid? Marise wailed, pushing past the young man, her devouring eyes seeming to snatch an impression of Valerie in one scouring instant and then dismiss it. —I forgot all about it. It can't be Wednesday already! Welcome home, honeypot. Give Mummy a million, million kisses. Give Jamie kisses. This is Jamie. Say hello. Isn't he sweet? Don't you remember him? He's in a band.

Dutifully Robyn said hello, gazing at Jamie without much interest and not moving to kiss anyone; her mother pounced in a cloud of perfume and carried her inside, calling back over her shoulder to Valerie in her husky voice, mistaking her for some sort of paid nanny, or pretending to. —Awfully nice of you. Are those her things? Do you want to drop her bags here in the hall? James can carry them up later. Do you have a cab? Or he can get you one. Oof, what a heavy big girl you're getting, Robby-bobby. Can you climb up on your own?

The hall was dim and high, lit by a feeble unshaded bulb; when determinedly Valerie followed after them, her heels echoed on black and white marble tiles. —Hello, Mrs. H, she sang out in her brightest telephone voice. —I'm the new Mrs. H. How nice to meet you.

Marise looked down at her from the curve of the staircase, where she was stooping over Robyn, setting her down. —Oh, I thought you might be. I'd thought he might have chosen someone like you.

—I'm hoping you're going to offer us a cup of tea, Valerie went on cheerfully. Of course Marise had known that she was bringing Robyn—Gil had telephoned last night to tell her. —Only we're frozen stiff, the pair of us! The heating on the train wasn't working, it's a disgrace.

—Do you take milk? Marise wondered. —Because I don't know if we have any milk.

—I don't mind so long as it's hot!

She submitted graciously when Jamie offered to take both bags, then was aware of his following her up the stairs, appraising her from behind, and thought that Marise was aware of it too. A wide door on the first floor, framed in ornamental plasterwork, stood open. You could see how once it had opened onto the best rooms at the heart of the whole house: now it had its own Yale lock and was painted purple and orange. The lower panels were dented and splintered as if someone had tried to kick through them. In the enormous room beyond there was a grey marble fireplace and a candelabra and floor-length windows hung with yellow brocade drapes, half-rotted; the glass in a vast gilt mirror was so foxed that it didn't double the perspective but closed it in, like a black fog. Valerie understood that, like the diamonds in Marise's hair, this wasn't really decaying aristocratic grandeur but an arty imitation of it. Marise led the way past a glass dome as tall as a man, filled with stuffed faded hummingbirds. A staring, dappled fairground horse had its flaring nostrils painted crimson; Robyn flinched from the horse as if from an old enemy. Fat old radiators under the windows were only lukewarm, but in the next room, which was smaller, a log fire burned in a stone grate, below a painting so darkened and dirty you could hardly make out a dead hare and brace of game birds. A sagging leather sofa, cushions cracked and pale with wear, spilled its horsehair innards in front of the fire. Jamie dropped the bags against a wall.

Robyn and Valerie, shivering in their coats, hung over the white ash in the grate as if it might be lifesaving, while Marise hunted for milk in what must be the kitchen next door, though it sounded cavernous; Jamie crouched to put on more logs, reaching his face towards the flame to reignite his rollie. The milk was off, Marise announced. There was a tin of tomato juice; wouldn't everyone prefer Bloody Marys? Rashly Valerie said that might be just the job, thinking she must pace herself, mustn't allow the drink to put her at any disadvantage. Again she felt herself observed, only this time it wasn't by Jamie, who had picked up a guitar and was sitting cross-legged on a goatskin rug, absorbed in messing about on the strings. Two mute figures, propped against the walls, glared with intensity—a carved African mask and a modern life-size woman made of something like varnished pink papier mâché, a caricatured nude with breasts pointed like torpedoes, the eyes and nipples and private parts in garish blue like a child's rude drawing. Valerie sat down in a corner of the sofa in her coat, knees carefully together.

The Bloody Marys when they came were strong, made with lots of Tabasco and ice and lemon and a stuffed olive on a stick: Marise said they were wonderfully nourishing, she lived on them. She even brought one—made without vodka, or only the tiniest teaspoonful—for Robyn, along with a packet of salted crisps. Kissing her, she pretended to gobble her up; Robyn submitted to the assault. —You're lucky, I saved those for you specially, I know that little girls are hungry bears. Because Jamie's a marauding bear too, he eats everything. I'll have to hide the food away, won't I, if we want to keep any of it for you. Are you still my hungry bear, Bobbin?

Robyn went unexpectedly then into a bear performance, hunching her shoulders, crossing her eyes, snuffling and panting, scrabbling in the air with her hands curled up like paws, her face a blunt little snout showing pointed teeth. They must have played this game before; Marise watched her daughter with distaste and pity, austere as a pillar in her white dress, fearsome and handsome as a carved ship's figurehead. For a moment Robyn really was a small, dull-furred brown bear, dancing joylessly to order. Valerie wouldn't have guessed that the child had it in her, to enter like this so completely into some other life than her own. In Valerie's own childhood she'd played imaginary games for hours on end with a gang of kids out on the bomb sites, pretending to be Red Indians on the trail, or pupils at a cruel boarding school, or prisoners escaping from the Germans. —Nice old bear, she said encouragingly.

—That's quite enough of that, Bobby, Marise said. —Most unsettling. Now why don't you go and play, darling? Take your crisps away before the Jamie-bear gets them.

Robyn returned into her ordinary self, faintly pink in the face. —Shall I show Auntie Valerie my bedroom?

Marise's eyes widened, ripe with scandal; she stared between Robyn and Valerie. —Auntie Valerie! Oho! What's this? Valerie isn't your real auntie, you know. Didn't anyone explain to you?

—We thought it was the best thing for her to call me, considering, Valerie said.

—Well, I'm relieved you didn't go in for *Mummy.* Or *Dearest Mamma,* or *Mom.*

Flustered, Robyn shot a guilty look at Valerie, as if she couldn't help letting her down. —I do know she's my stepmother really.

—That's better. Your *wicked* stepmother, don't forget. Marise winked broadly at Valerie. —Now off you go. She doesn't want to see your bedroom.

They heard Robyn trail through the kitchen, open another door on the far side, close it again behind her. The fire blazed up, Jamie began picking out something on his guitar, Marise rescued his rollie from the ashtray and fell with it into the opposite end of the sofa. Valerie guessed that they were smoking pot—that was what the zoo smell was. She thought that she ought to leave, there was nothing for her here, she had made her point coming inside. —So Valerie, Marise said musingly. —How did you get on with my dear daughter? Funny little snake, isn't she? I hope Gilbert enjoyed spending every moment with her, after all those protestations of how he's such a devoted father. Was she a good girl?

—Awfully good. We didn't have a squeak of trouble.

—I mean, isn't she just a piece of Gilbert? Except not clever of course. Poor little mite, with his looks and my brains.

Outside the last of the afternoon light was being blotted out, and although wind buffeted the loose old windowpanes, no one stirred to draw the curtains or switch on the lamps. Valerie wanted to go, but the drink was stronger than she was used to, and the heat from the fire seemed to press her down in the sofa. Also, obscurely she feared returning in the dusk through the next room, past the stuffed birds and that horse. Succumbing to the music as it gathered force, she was imagining how her husband might have been impressed and excited once by this careless, shameless, disordered household. If you owned so much, you could afford to trample it underfoot in a grand gesture, turning everything into a game.

—I do adore clever men, Marise went on. —I was so in love with Gilbert's intelligence, absolutely crazy about him at first. I could sit listening to him for hours on end, telling me all about history and ideas and art. Because, you know, I'm just an absolute idiot, I was kicked out of school when I was fourteen. The nuns hated me: Valerie, truly, I can hardly read and write. Whereas I expect you can do typing and shorthand, you clever girl. So I'd just kneel there at Gilbert's feet gazing up at him while he talked. You know, just talking, talking, droning on and on. So pleased with himself. Don't men just love that?

—Do they? I wouldn't know.

—But they do, they love it when we're kneeling at their feet. Jamie thinks that's hilarious, don't you Jamie? Because now I'm worshipping him instead, he thinks. Worshipping his guitar.

—My talent, Jamie chastely suggested. Marise shuffled down in the sofa to poke her white boot at him, prodding at his hands and blocking the strings so that he couldn't play until he ducked the arm of his guitar out of her way. His exasperated look slid past her teasing and onto Valerie, where it rested. Marise subsided with a sigh. —So Gilbert's sitting there steering along in the little cockpit of his own cleverness, believing himself so shining, such a wonder! And then suddenly one day I couldn't stand it! I thought—but the whole *world*, the whole of real life, is spread out underneath him. And he's up there all alone above the skies, in his own clever head. Don't you know what I mean?

—I've never taken much interest in Gil's work, Valerie said primly. —Though of course I'm aware how highly it's regarded. I've got my own interests.

—Oh, have you? Good for you! Because I've never really had any interests to speak of. I've counted on the men in my life to supply those. Gilbert was certainly interesting. Did you know that he beat me? Yes, really. To a pulp, my dear.

What melodrama! Valerie laughed out loud, she didn't

believe it. Or perhaps she did. When Marise, mocking, blew out a veil of smoke and left a thick print of plum lipstick on the cigarette, she had a glimpse for a moment of Gil's malevolent Bitch-from-hell, the strong-jawed dark sorceress who might incite a man to violence. Poor Gilbert. And it was true that his rages had been a revelation when they were first married. In the university office, all the women had petted him and worshipped his mystique: he had seemed thoughtful, forgetful, bumbling, dryly humorous and high-minded. She stood up, trying to shake off the influence of the Bloody Mary. Her mother would be expecting her, she said. —And I don't know what your plans are for Robyn's tea. But I made us cheese sandwiches for the train, so she's had a decent lunch at least, and an apple and a Mars bar.

Marise was amused. —I don't have any plans for Robyn's tea. I've never really made those kind of plans.

She stretched out, luxuriating into the extra space on the sofa, putting her boots up, her eyes glassy in their pits of shadow. Valerie meant to go looking for Robyn then, to say goodbye, but the sight of chaos in the kitchen brought her up short: dishes piled in an old sink, gas cooker filthy with grease, torn slices of bread and stained tea towels and orange peel lying around on the linoleum floor where they'd been dropped. The table was still laid with several plates where some dark meat stew or rich sauce was congealing. She went to pick up her bag instead. —Give her my love, she said.

—Oh, Robyn won't remember, said Marise.

No one offered to show Valerie out. Heroically, like a girl in a film, she made her way alone through the next-door room, where the pale horse gleamed sinisterly; she startled at a movement which might have been the flutter of stuffed birds, but was only her own reflection in the foxed mirror. On the stairs she remembered that she shouldn't have called it tea. Gil was always reminding her to say dinner, or sometimes supper. And once she was outside on the path in the wind Valerie looked back, searching along the first-floor windows of the house for any sign of the child looking out. But it was impossible to see, the glass was reflecting a last smouldering streak of sunset, dark as a livid coal smashed open in a fire.

THAT NIGHT IT SNOWED. VALERIE WOKE UP IN THE MORNING in her old bedroom at her mother's and knew it before she even looked outside: a purer, weightless light bloomed on the wallpaper, and all the crowded muddle of gloomy furniture inherited from her grandmother seemed washed clean and self-explanatory. She opened the curtains and lay looking out at the snow falling, exhilarated as if she were back inside her childhood. Her mother had the wireless on downstairs.

—Trains aren't running, she said gloatingly when Valerie came down; she was sitting smoking at the table in her house-coat, in the heat of the gas fire. Everything was odd, light was blocked which should have come through the corrugated plastic roof over the yard. —So I suppose you'll have to stay over another night.

—Oh, I don't know, Mum. I've got things to do at home.

The snow made her restless; she didn't want to be shut up with her mother all day with nothing to talk about. She found a pair of zip-up sheepskin boots at the back of a cupboard and ventured out to the phone box. Front doors in the narrow street opened directly onto the pavement; snow was blowing across in wafting veils, and the quiet was like a sudden deafness. Breaking into the crusted surface her boots creaked. No one had come out to shovel yet, nothing was spoiled, a few parked cars were mounded with white, every least horizontal ledge and edge and rim was capped with exquisite delicacy. The phone box was smothered in snow and the light was blue-grey inside it. She pushed her money in and called Gil, told him she was going to the station to find out what was happening. He said there was snow in the North too; he wouldn't go in to the faculty meeting today, he'd work on his book at home. —Please try to get here any way you can, he said in a low urgent voice. —He misses you.

—I have to go, she said. —There's quite a queue outside.

But there wasn't, there was only silence and the shifting vacancy; the footprints she'd made on her way were filling up already, almost erased. —I don't know why you're so eager to get back to him, her mother grumbled. But Valerie wasn't really thinking about Gil: it was the strangeness of the snow she liked, and the disruption it caused. It took her almost an hour and a half to get to King's Cross—the Underground was working, but it was slow. When she surfaced it had stopped snowing, at least for the moment, but there still weren't any trains; a porter said she should try again later that afternoon—it was his guess that if the weather held they might be able to reopen some of the major routes. Valerie didn't want to linger in King's Cross. She put her bag in left luggage, then thought of going shopping after all—they'd surely have cleared Oxford Street. But she took the Piccadilly line instead, as far as South Ken. By the time she arrived at the Chelsea house it was gone two o'clock.

The house was almost unrecognisable at first, transformed in the snow. It seemed exposed and taller and more formidable, more mysteriously separated from its neighbours, standing apart in dense shrubbery—which was half-obliterated under its burden of white. Valerie didn't even know why she'd come back. Perhaps she'd had some idea that if she saw Marise today she'd be able somehow to behave with more sophistication, say what she really thought. As she arrived at the corner she glanced up at the side windows on the first floor. And there was Robyn looking out—in the wrong direction at first, so that she didn't see Valerie. She seemed to be crouched on the windowsill, slumped against the glass—it was unmistakeably her, because although it was past lunchtime she was still dressed in the new white pyjamas.

Valerie stopped short in her tramping. Her boots were wet through. Had she seriously entertained an idea of ringing the doorbell and being invited inside again, without any decent pretext, into that place where she most definitely wasn't wanted? The next moment it was too late: Robyn had seen her. The child's whole body responded in a violent spasm of astonishment, almost as if she'd been looking out for Valerie, yet not actually expecting her to appear. In the whole week of her visit, she'd never reacted so forcefully to anything. She leaped up on the windowsill, waving frantically, so that she was pressed full length against the glass. Remembering how those windows had rattled the night before, Valerie signalled to her to get down, motioning with her gloved hand and mouthing. Robyn couldn't hear her but gazed in an intensity of effort at comprehension. Valerie signalled crossly again: get down, be careful. Robyn shrugged, then gestured eagerly down to the front door, miming opening something. Valerie saw she didn't have a choice. Nodding and pointing, she agreed that she was on her way round to the front. No one had trodden yet in the snow along the path, but she was lucky, the front entrance had been left open—deliberately perhaps, because as she stepped into the hall a man called out, low-voiced and urgent, from the top landing. —John, is that you?

Apologising into the dimness for not being John, Valerie hurried upstairs to where Robyn was fumbling with latches on the other side of the purple and orange door. Then she heard Jamie. —Hullo! Now what are you up to? Is someone out there?

Valerie saw when the door swung back that—alarmingly—Jamie was in his underpants. He was bemused rather than hostile. —What are you doing here?

She invented hastily, hot-faced, avoiding looking at his near-nakedness. —Robyn forgot something, I came to give it to her.

—I want to show her my toys, Robyn said.

Jamie hesitated. —Her mother's lying down, she's got a headache. But you might as well come in. There's no one else for her to play with.

Robyn pulled Valerie by the hand through a door which led straight into the kitchen; someone had cleared up those plates of stew, but without scraping them—they were stacked beside the sink. The only sign of breakfast was an open packet of cornflakes on the table, and a bowl and spoon. In Robyn's bedroom, across a short passageway, there really were nice toys, better than anything Valerie had ever possessed: a dolls' house, a dolls' cradle with white muslin drapes, a wooden Noah's Ark whose roof lifted off. A frieze was painted in pastel colours above the picture rail, the Pied Piper leading a dance of enchanted children. The room was cold and cheerless though, and there were no sheets on the bare mattress, only a dirty yellow nylon sleeping bag. No one had unpacked Robyn's suitcase, everything was still folded inside—she must have opened it herself to get out her pyjamas. The drawers in a chest were hanging open and most of Robyn's clothes seemed to be overflowing from plastic shopping bags piled against the walls.

—I knew you'd come back, Robyn earnestly said, not letting go of Valerie's hand.

Valerie opened her mouth to explain that it was only because she'd missed her train in all this weather, then she changed her mind. —We weren't expecting snow, were we? she said brightly.

—Have you come to get me? Are you taking me to your house again?

She explained that she'd only come to say goodbye.

—No, please don't say goodbye! Auntie Valerie, don't go.

—I'm sure you'll be coming to stay with us again soon.

Convulsively the child flung against her, butting with her head. —Not soon, now. I want to come now!

Robyn was almost more likeable with her face screwed

into an ugly fury, suffused with red, kicking out with her feet, the placid brushstrokes of her brows distorted to exclamation marks. Holding her off by her shoulders, Valerie felt the after-tremor of her violence.

—Do you really want to come home with me?

—Really, really, Robyn pleaded.

—But what about your mummy?

—She won't mind! We can get out without her noticing.

—Oh, I think we'll need to talk to her. But let's pack first. And you have to get dressed—if you're really sure, that is. We need to go back to the station to see if the trains are running.

Valerie looked around with a new purposefulness, assessing quickly. —Where's your coat? Do you need the bathroom? Have you cleaned your teeth?

Robyn sat abruptly on the floor to take off her pyjamas, and Valerie tipped out the contents of the suitcase, began repacking it with a few things that looked useful, underwear and wool jumpers and shoes. The toothbrush was still in its sponge bag. Then they heard voices, and a chair knocked over in the kitchen, and before Valerie could prepare what she ought to say, Marise came stalking into the bedroom with Jamie behind her. At least he had put on his trousers. Wrapped in a gold silk kimono embroidered with dragons, the sooty remnants of yesterday's make-up under her eyes, her dark hair hanging loose almost to her waist, Marise looked as formidable as a tragic character in a play.

—How remarkable! she exclaimed. —What do you think you're doing, Valerie? Are you kidnapping my child?

—Don't be ridiculous, Valerie coolly said. —I'm not kidnapping anyone. I was about to come and find you, to ask
whether she could come back with us for another week or so.
And I've got a perfect right anyway. She says that she'd prefer
to be at her father's.

—I'm calling the police.

—I wouldn't if I were you. You haven't got a leg to stand
on. It's criminal neglect. Look at this room! There aren't even
sheets on her bed.

—She prefers a sleeping bag. Ask her!

Frozen in the act of undressing, Robyn turned her face,
blank with dismay, back and forward between the two women.

—And I'd like to know, Valerie said, —what she's eaten
since she came home. There isn't any milk in the house, is
there? It's two thirty in the afternoon and all the child has had
since lunchtime yesterday is dry cornflakes.

—You know nothing about motherhood, nothing! Marise
shrieked. —Robyn won't touch milk, she hates it. She's been
fussy from the day she was born. And she's a spy, she's a little
spy! Telling tales about me. How dare she? She's a vicious un-
grateful little snake and you've encouraged her in it. I knew
this would happen. I should never have let Gilbert take her in
the first place, I knew he'd only be stirring her up against me.
Where's he been all these years, with his so-called feelings for
his daughter, I'd like to know? Jamie, get this kidnapping cheap
whore out of here, won't you? No, I like whores. She's much
worse, she's a *typist*.

·   ·   ·

VALERIE SAID THAT SHE DIDN'T NEED JAMIE TO TAKE HER ANY-
where, and that if they were slinging names about, she knew
what Marise was. Minutes later, she was standing outside
in the garden, stopping to catch her breath beside the gate,
where the dustbins—each with its lid of snow—were set back
from the path behind a screen of pines. She was smitten with
the cold and trembling, penitent and ashamed. She shouldn't
have interfered, she was out of her depth. It was true that she
didn't know anything about motherhood. Hadn't she encouraged Robyn just as Marise said, trying to make the child like
her? And without genuinely liking in return. Now she had
abandoned her to her mother's revenge, which might be awful.
Then the front door opened and Jamie was coming down the
path, with a curious exulting look on his face: in his arms,
clasped against his bare chest, he was carrying the dirty yellow
sleeping bag that had been on Robyn's bed. Hustling Valerie
back among the pines, out of sight of the windows, he dumped
the bag at her feet. —Off you go, he said significantly, as if
he and Valerie were caught up in some game together. —Her
mother's lying down again. Take your chance and get out of
here.

It took her a moment or two to understand. In the meantime he'd returned inside the house and closed the door. There
was a mewing from the bag, she fumbled to unroll it, and
Robyn struggled out from inside, wrapping her arms, with a
fierce sigh of submission, around Valerie's knees. But she was
in her white pyjamas, barefoot, in the snow! How could they
make their way through the streets with Robyn dressed like
that? A window opened above them and Jamie lobbed out

something, which landed with a soft thud on the path. It was one of the bags from Robyn's room, packed with a miscellany of clothes—and he'd thought to add the pair of plimsolls too. Then he closed the window and disappeared. There was no coat in the bag, but never mind. In panicking haste Valerie helped Robyn put on layers of clothes over her pyjamas: socks, cord trousers, plimsolls, jumper.

—I thought he was going to eat me, Robyn said.

—Don't be silly, Valerie reassured her firmly. She kicked the sleeping bag away out of sight, among the hedge-roots.

—Are we escaping?

—We're having an adventure.

And they set out, ducking into the street, hurrying along beside the hedge; Robyn's plimsolls were sodden in moments. By a lucky chance, as soon as they got to the main road there was a taxi nosing through the slush. —How much to King's Cross? Valerie asked. She had all the money she'd been saving up to spend on a new dress; she'd have to buy Robyn a train ticket too. Then she asked the taxi to stop at a post office, where she went inside to send a telegram. She couldn't tele-phone Gil; she knew he'd forbid her to bring the child back again. But she couldn't arrive with Robyn without warning him. "Returning with daughter," she wrote out on the form. "No fit home for her here." She counted out the shillings from her purse.

Back in the taxi, making conversation, she asked Robyn where her dollies were. Robyn was stricken, she'd forgot-ten them, left them behind under her pillow. It was dusk in the streets already: as they drove on, the coloured lights from the shops wheeled slowly across their faces, revealing them as strangers to each other. Valerie was thinking that she might need to summon all this effort of ingenuity one day for some escape of her own, dimly imagined, and that taking on the child made her less free. Robyn sat forward on the seat, tensed with her loss. Awkwardly Valerie tried putting an arm around her, to reassure her. She said not to worry, they would make new dolls, and better ones. Just for the moment, though, the child was inconsolable.

Men

AT ABOUT SEVEN O'CLOCK A CROWD CAME IN. THEY WERE
booked for an overnight, and dinner in the Jazz Bar—the
men were loud and middle-aged, they had money and stood
at ease in the foyer in their business suits, as if they owned
the place. Strong, confident accents from across the Pennines,
Leeds or Sheffield. The women varied: some of them were
obviously first wives, hanging on from another less prosperous
era, solid and plain and mouthy, mothers of grown children,
packed pugnaciously into expensive tight dresses and lethal
heels, defying the showy hotel. Other men had shed their
first wives and acquired a newer model, younger and slimmer,
promising a dream of sex; these new girls were either full of
themselves, or diffidently shy. The ringleader among the men
was a clever talker, short, with a paunch and thick nut-brown
hair, bald patch like a monk's; his ugliness was attractive, with
his blue eyes shifting quickly from face to face, entertaining
his companions, making sure they were all on board with his
jokes, his know-how. He charmed them all, touching every-

one with his quick hands, bringing them inside his magic circle, even the dumpiest of the old wives. And his girl stood out, she was different: very tall and serene, and pale—not like the others with their Lanzarote tans. She wore a long tasteful pastel dress, not split up to her thigh or cut to show off her breasts—though you noticed the shape of her breasts, loose under the loose fabric. Her hair was old-gold colour, silky, a good cut, feathered onto her white shoulders. She smiled around her as if she wasn't afraid of anything, and her smile didn't change when the bald-patch man trailed fingers down her back, between the shoulder blades; she was still free. He was talking away to the others at the same time, telling some old story about his great-grandfather who'd fought and won against a rival in this city once, at Moran's Boxing Booth, famous in those days.

Michelle Brennan came through from the staff area into the space behind the reception desk, bumping the swing door open with her behind, preoccupied, holding her bookings chart in both hands and frowning down at it. There was some minor glitch with this block booking which she was worrying over. Then she thought that she was aware of her sister's presence instantly, vividly, even before she looked up, like an animal picking up a scent, a smear of something rank; yet she hadn't seen her for fifteen years, not since Jan was seventeen. And as soon as she'd seized an image of her, in one swooping, rapacious glance—the serenity and the thinness and the beauty and the dress and the man—she looked away again, back to her paper, and pretended she hadn't seen. No one else would have noticed anything. There wasn't any resemblance between the two sisters. Michelle wasn't beautiful, she looked like their mother, small and dark with a little pasty face as soft as putty. Their father had been the tall fair one, good-looking, a fine waste of space.

As far as Michelle knew, staring down at her chart, unable to see anything for a few moments, Jan never once looked over in the direction of the reception desk. Though it must have occurred to her, surely, however serene she was, that Michelle might well still be working here, where their mother had worked before her: unless it was really that easy to forget everything. Michelle soon saw how to resolve her booking problem—upgrade one of the party to a suite on the second floor, no one ever objected to that. They'd had a cancellation earlier. She helped one of the receptionists put this change into the system, went back through the swing door to her office. Later she asked Paul, the sales manager who knew everyone, about the crowd in the Jazz Bar. —Somebody's fiftieth, he said. —The little fella.

—And who's he when he's at home?

—Architectural salvage. Smart guy. Started out in waste management. Somebody's got to do it.

When she googled him it turned out that Martin Donoghue was in property development too, and urban landscaping: on his website there were photographs of old red-brick mills like the ones where her uncles and her grandparents and great-grandparents had once slaved their lives away, turned now into expensive flats, among the canals which didn't run with poisonous dyes any longer, and were planted with wild flowers. So that was how Jan lived.

·   ·   ·

IN THE JAZZ BAR THEY WERE A NOISY CROWD, BUT THERE wasn't any trouble. You never knew, all that testosterone kicking around and the men showing off their girls, the senior wives on edge and combative, the drink running freely. You didn't get to make a fortune starting off in waste management, and be a pussycat. But Jack, who was head of security, took one look at the party and wasn't worried. Jack was a big man, an ex-wrestler like the security guy before him, he was a rock, he knew all the people Paul said he wished he didn't have to know. Martin Donoghue was all right, he was a sophisticated operator, it wasn't just a veneer. He was paying for everything on his card, there was no flashing wads of cash around. And he took care of everyone round the table, calling them by name as if he were coaxing them and herding them in the direction he wanted, remembering the names and ages of all their children and even their grandchildren, keeping up the flow of his jokes and cajoling the whole time. —Don't be shy, ladies! Go for a bit of what you fancy, a nice T-bone. Any requests, send to the piano, but keep it clean. Boys, did you see the game on Saturday? Tidy player, but no finishing skills. A man's got to know how to finish what he started, isn't that right?

Courteously he asked the waitress what she was studying at college, encouraged her to apply herself to her subject and not lose heart. He made sure that some of the older folk—the ones his own age or more, who were maybe a bit rougher round the edges—weren't made to feel foolish when it came to ordering from the menu. Subtly he helped them choose, without their noticing. —You like a nice piece of salmon, don't you, John? Why don't you try it with a sauce?

Ordering the wine—champagne for anyone who wanted it, he'd rather drink a decent red himself—he seemed to know what he was talking about. He made them all feel that they belonged there in the hotel, they had rights to it.

—My mum used to work in here, Jan said suddenly, as if she were amazed at it herself. —When I was a little girl. I don't mean in this bar. She just cleaned the rooms.

Martin didn't seem to think this shamed them, he was delighted. —You're kidding me. Why didn't you tell me?

—I'd forgotten which hotel it was, until just now.

It was a surprise to some of them that she had an ordinary past at all, let alone here in this city, and cleaning; they'd imagined for some reason, feeling hostility because of her looks and dreamy detachment, that she must come from the alien South. Though now she'd told them, it was obvious, you could hear it in her voice. —She used to bring us in sometimes, Jan said, —me and my sister, when she couldn't find anyone to mind us. The housekeeper let her put us in a room if one was empty, we had to watch telly and not touch anything. I loved it. I used to pretend I lived here and it was my palace.

—And now it is your palace, my darling, Martin said.

Some of the women knew Martin's wife, who'd been in and out of psychiatric hospital for years, from long before Jan was on the scene. He wouldn't divorce Kay, because for one thing he was sentimentally attached to his religion—although who knew when Martin Donoghue last stepped inside a church? At any rate, he wore his St. Christopher on a gold chain round his neck: with his top button undone, you saw it nestling in the fuzz of grey hair on his chest. As for Jan, she wasn't quick with her repartee, wasn't funny like some of the other women or like Kay was, on her good days—and she didn't have kids, so they weren't sure how to talk to her. She could discuss make-up and clothes, but her elegance made them uneasy; she'd done some modelling, she said. I'll bet you have, the women thought. But they also thought that Martin deserved his fun, if she was his idea of fun.

He'd insisted on breaking up the couples around the table in the fashionable way, and been careful to seat himself between Kath and Gerry, his oldest friends from his Harehills past, where he could make sure they didn't feel lost, or pick fights with each other or with anyone. Gerry looked twenty years older than him, though they'd been in the same class at school— not that they'd attended very often; Gerry was missing half his teeth because he was too stubborn or too much afraid to go to the dentist, though Martin had offered a hundred times to pay. And Kath had been a nice-looking woman once; she was as skinny as ever and good in a dress, but the drink was a blank in her face even when she was scrubbed up like tonight, with her hair tied back neatly in a ribbon. Kath and Gerry both had a weakness for drink, they couldn't handle it.

From time to time across the table Martin exchanged a look with Jan, or said something to attract her attention. You could see how he enjoyed having her there, balancing his heat and his energy with her calm. It didn't worry him that she didn't talk much. There was an affinity between them, only not in words. Jan wasn't highly intelligent, Martin thought, but she had something else which was just as good, or better: she floated out of reach of all the taking offence and nursing grudges and feuding which had been the atmosphere of his childhood and youth. Jan had told him that she'd taken a lot of drugs at one point, and been pretty crazy at the time. But there wasn't a sign of any damage, to look at her. She was always as cool as if she'd dropped into his life from another world. Or from another planet, a planet where all the women were six foot tall and the light was different, clear and green.

MICHELLE DIDN'T WANT TO TAKE EVEN ONE PEEK INTO THE Jazz Bar. She was on late but she kept out of the way, found things to do in the office instead of taking a turn on reception. She spent half her life in that scruffy old office which smelled of the food compressor; Paul said that it would have suited her in the old days when the staff lived in, sharing rooms on the top floor. Michelle was divorced, she didn't have much to go home for now that her daughter was away at university. And then as fate would have it, just at the very moment when she happened to push through the swing door to the front of house, the Donoghue party came out of the bar to go up to bed. Last ones out, naturally: suit jackets off now and shirtsleeves rolled up, Rolex watches flashing on hairy arms, back-slapping, shouted farewells on their way upstairs as if it weren't past midnight already, mock-fights getting into the lift, those women shrieking with laughter and cursing at the top of their voices. Her sister was draped around Martin Donoghue, who was glad-handing everyone, the whole evening his demonstration of what money could buy. Usually Michelle enjoyed coming out from the workaday reality behind the scenes, into the foyer with its seventeen different types of marble, its chandeliers and pink Peterhead granite floor. But tonight all the good tone of the place was spoiled.

Jan seemed to lift her head to look back from where she leant against Martin, the two of them the last ones waiting by the lifts; she was scanning vaguely around the foyer as though in search of someone, but without much expectation of seeing them. And then perhaps she did actually catch sight of Michelle: who had her head bent down by this time, peering assiduously into one of the screens on reception. Didn't Jan seem to straighten up in excitement? Puzzling as if she couldn't be certain, but might break off at any moment and hurry over towards her sister, calling out to her. Michelle only turned away, as if she hadn't noticed anything. Pushing back through the swing door she returned to work, and no one came following after her.

For a long while everything was quiet in the sleeping hotel. But Michelle was so keyed up she couldn't get on with anything properly, couldn't see what was in front of her on her screen; she was fumbling, folding invoices into their envelopes. She ought to call her taxi and go home, but felt as if she were waiting for something to happen, a storm to break. Then just after one o'clock came the call from security she must have been dreading—or half-desiring, because it would reveal at last how things really were. Someone had reported

noises of a domestic in the suite on the second floor. Following Jack upstairs, in the well-rehearsed quick bustle of their
emergency response—it was policy to have female staff present
for support—Michelle hugged her vindication painfully to her
chest. Wasn't she anticipating Jan weeping and holding a towel
to her face, bright red with blood? Or carried out from the
suite on a stretcher? Or underneath a sheet? Hurrying after
Jack in the airless corridor, her imagination was like her own
violence breaking out at last.

But after all that, it was only a false alarm. Martin Donoghue hadn't taken the suite for himself, he'd put a couple of his
friends in there, the roughest old types of drinker: Michelle had
taken good note of them downstairs. And in fact Donoghue
was already on the scene by the time they got there, calming
things down and reproaching his friends and apologising for
them, closing the door on their bleary disgrace: it looked as
though the old chap had got the worst of it. —They're an
awful old pair, he said to Jack and Michelle ruefully, sotto voce
in the corridor, tucking his twenty-pound notes discreetly into
Jack's top pocket. —But you know, they're old friends, what
can you do? I couldn't cut them out, on a special occasion. But
I'm very sorry for the disturbance. They'll be meek as lambs
from now on, I promise you.

He was in his white towelling gown, as if he'd come from
the shower, or from his bed—one of those stocky men who
seem to give off heat like an engine, with their thrumming
chest voices, so sure of their power to always smooth the way
ahead of them. Michelle was close enough to smell the drink
on him, and the cologne; he gripped Jack's huge hand confi-

dently when he shook it, and she knew that if she'd given him her hand he was the type to put it to his lips and kiss it, or try to get round her in some other way. So she kept both hands behind her back, unsmiling, standing apart from the whole exchange between him and Jack there in the corridor as if she were dull as a plain pudding, with nothing to say for herself. She'd have liked to tell Martin Donoghue what she thought of his whole party and their behaviour, but knew she mustn't. She was there as a representative of the ethos of the hotel.

AS A SPECIAL FAVOUR, ON DAYS WHEN THEIR MOTHER HAD TO bring Michelle and Jan to the hotel, the housekeeper would let her know which rooms were finished with. Then the girls were shut in with daytime telly and a bottle of Coke each, and a bag of sweets; Michelle was in charge because she was seven years older. They were supposed to sit still where they were and not touch anything, but of course they did touch. They loved the silky perfect spacious rooms where nothing was spoiled or dirty or belonged to anyone. Michelle was good at inventing games, and they had favourite ones they only ever played on hotel days. Princess Time was like a TV show, they lounged around languidly combing each other's hair and painting their mouths with red sweets, taking it in turn to be the servant. Or there was Holy Book, involving the Gideon Bible from the drawer in the bedside table. Michelle opened it at random, reading out from it or pretending to—Jan wouldn't have known the difference, she always had problems with her reading. Whatever the Book told them, they had to do: even if it was sitting with a bare bum on the toilet while the other one flushed, or putting shampoo on their tongues out of the little bottles.

Michelle had a job keeping everything intact, in case the housekeeper or their mother looked in to check on them. Jan wasn't dreamy or serene as a little girl. She was funny-looking, with a wide gap-toothed grin and sticking-out ears, and she was a wild thing—though Michelle knew it was partly her own fault, working her up to such excitement in the games. She had to run round after her sister, sweeping crisp crumbs from the carpet or smoothing out the bedcover if Jan had leaped on it, mopping up in the bathroom when Jan turned on the shower, rearranging the towels perfectly afterwards with the wet inside, praying no one would notice. When their mother had finished work she checked all round to see if they'd left traces, but never found them, except that she refolded the ends of the toilet paper. —Good girls, she admired them, in her dispirited, worn-out way. —What good girls I've got.

And then as they went down in the service lift Jan would nudge Michelle behind their mother's back, opening her hand with its sticky pink fat fingers and quickly clamping it shut again, showing exultantly on her palm whatever it was she'd stolen this time: a mending kit or strands torn from the tassel on the curtain tie-back, nuts from the minibar or a miniature soap in its waxed wrapping. Once—most awfully—it was a page torn out from the Holy Book, folded into a hot tight square. Michelle scolded her bitterly when they were alone. Didn't she know, she could get them into such trouble? Their mother would lose her job. But Jan wouldn't give up whatever her latest treasure was. With her secretive sly look she twisted out of Michelle's way, doubling over in the backyard where they played and hunching her shoulders to protect herself, holding out stubbornly against her sister's prising, punishing fingers and her blows. And Jan didn't even want to keep those stolen things! She would give them away happily to just anyone: the worst girls in the playground at school, who only ever laughed at her old rubbish, or kids she met playing on the street and never saw again.

MICHELLE WASN'T ON UNTIL ONE THE NEXT DAY. SHE'D thought that the Donoghue crowd would all be long gone by the time she arrived, but apparently he'd had a late checkout and she'd only just missed them. Sunita on reception informed her that Mrs. Donoghue had asked for her by name. —By name indeed! And who's Mrs. Donoghue, I wonder?

Sunita had told Mrs. D that she could leave a note but she'd said not to worry, and Michelle could just imagine why: Jan's writing wasn't up to much, she couldn't spell and she muddled up the capitals and small letters, made her numbers backwards. At school she'd had special classes but they didn't help. Michelle knew all about this because after their mother died, when Michelle's own daughter was still a baby, she'd taken Jan in and tried to be a second mother to her. Until Jan ran away when she was seventeen.

She went upstairs to talk to the housekeeper: there were a few late checkouts to cover, some earlies coming in. On her way down, on an impulse, she let herself in with her master key to the room where Jan had stayed with Martin Donoghue. She knocked first and her heart beat as if she expected to find them still inside, caught out in something, half-undressed, or leering at her from the bed. And the state of the room was shocking. You learned a lot about people from the way they left a hotel room. Sheets stained with wine were dragged off the bed halfway across the carpet, muddled up with a mess of eggshells and greasy leftovers on their breakfast tray. Broken pieces of a wine glass were dark with dregs, there were used teabags posted at intervals like someone's joke along the windowsill, sodden towels smeared with foundation and mascara were dropped all over the floor in the bedroom and bathroom, everything stank of scent and sweat. The drain in the shower was clogged, an empty shampoo bottle floated in scummy water. Some things don't change, then, Michelle grimly thought.

With half an hour to spare, she might as well sort out this lot before anyone else saw, in case they ever knew it was her sister. She turned on the air conditioning; borrowing a trolley, she brought clean linen and with quick accustomed hands began putting everything back in order, stripping the bed, wearing rubber gloves to scrabble the longer fair hairs and soapy twist of short dark hairs from the plughole in the shower, spraying around with cleanser, restoring the rooms to pristine nothingness. There was usually something satisfying in such work; only today she was tense with expectation, as if she were looking for something under all the mess. There must be some clue in here, some message left for her. She even found herself searching in the waste bins, through the used dirty cotton buds and dental floss and empty blister pack of paracetamol—

unwrapping screwed-up scraps of paper and reading through them. Nothing of interest: receipts from a motorway café and a taxi, a request from a charity, a list of scribbled figures, not in Jan's hand. Like a madwoman, she thought. That was what Jan had said to her years ago, when she found Michelle going through the things in her bedroom once, looking for traces. —*You're mad,* Jan furiously said. —I don't even know what it is you're looking for. Traces of what?

There was nothing in this hotel room anyway to show that Jan wasn't perfectly happy. Whatever Michelle was looking for, her sister had taken it away with her.

Cecilia Awakened

CECILIA AWAKENED FROM HER CHILDHOOD ON HOLIDAY IN
Italy, the summer she was fifteen. It was not a sexual awak-
ening, or not exactly—rather an intellectual or imaginative
one. Until that summer, the odd child she was had fitted in
perfectly with the oddity of her rather elderly parents. Her
father worked in a university library and her mother wrote
historical novels, and when they had come late to marriage—
and then to childbearing and child-rearing—they had seen
no reason to change the entrenched patterns of their lives, or
become more like ordinary people. No one who knew them
could quite think afterwards how they had managed nappies
and dummies and spooning in baby food. They couldn't really
remember themselves, how they had managed it. A squalling
small baby must have been an eruption of anarchy in lives that
were otherwise characterised by restraint and irony.

It was only the once, anyway. There was only Cecilia, and
she didn't squall for long.

Even when her father was still carrying her in a backpack,

she had looked around her with those wise huge eyes that were like her mother's, pale and pink-lidded, drinking everything in with appetite and wondering at it, but not participating. Soon she had learned to hate children's parties, preferring a trip to a museum or a castle—or rambling in the Lake District, pressing flowers for her collection. She had a stamp collection too, and she and her father made what he called "stinks" with a chemistry set—although she quickly knew, she said, that science "wasn't her thing." By the time she was nine she had read *Middlemarch* and most of Dickens; she learned the violin and played it scratchily but at a tremendous pace, advancing through all the grades; finicky over her food, for years she was miniature, like an elf or a wizened old woman. She took extra Latin lessons at school because it helped her grasp the roots of her own language; her teachers encouraged her and showed her off but didn't like her, with her curious mixture of assurance and shy clumsiness. Cecilia wasn't afraid of adults in those days, only of other children. At puberty suddenly she grew tall and got an appetite, her limbs and her waist thickened, her skin was waxy and her hair which had been fair turned to mud-brown. She was affronted by this bodily assault; discreetly her mother, Angela, supplied her with sanitary pads. Mother and daughter conferred only briefly and abruptly about such facts of life. Female biology seemed a disenchantment, after Cecilia's pure childhood.

Still, the biology had produced Cecilia, and she was a marvel. If her parents mourned the fey little sprite she had been, they loved her too tenderly to give her the least sign of it. The three of them did everything together, they liked the same things and shared the same jokes: most of all, they liked the past. It was as if the past in some sense belonged to them, because they knew about it and understood it, whereas in the present they were submerged among so many alien others, such hostile cross-currents, in such oceans of what was crass and wrong. You could feel their relief when they stepped apart from the crowd in the high street of some provincial English town, spoiled by its Poundworld and its McDonald's and iden-tikit shabby chain stores, into the embracing quiet of some Tudor or Georgian house open to the public, where a ticket seller dozed behind a few faded postcards. They even regretted it if the National Trust got hold of such a place and jazzed it up. Try on the crinoline, the wig! See if you can write a poem like Coleridge's! The more austere the history to be digested the better, so far as Ken, Cecilia's father, was concerned. Angela teased that he was never happier than when he spotted dense information boards, complete with floor plans, colour-coded for different historical periods. She and Cecilia preferred a family tree, finding out which haughty beauty in a portrait married whom, which children died tragically young.

Angela was dreamy when she got up close to the past: perhaps on the trail of something, a new story to write. She liked to close her eyes, breathe in the smell of a place and feel its ghosts around her. In her own childhood, she had read so many books in which a house's past was actually alive in the next room: you had only to open the right door to come across the Edwardian children who'd lived there once, or the Tudor plotters, or some powdered jaded aristocrat bent over his papers or her embroidery. Reading aloud to Cecilia when she was small, Angela had loved re-entering into the spirit of these old books, and was sometimes so absorbed that she went on reading long after Cecilia had fallen asleep. Of course it had to be an old house for the time travel to work. Angela had resented, when she was growing up, the smart homes her parents preferred, their showy rooms all window, their roots so shallowly planted in history. She had yearned to own somewhere with a priest's hole; or an attic at least, with a trunk full of yellowed letters and long dresses. In real life, needless to say, she and Ken had had to make do with less, but she'd held out for a brick-built cottage in Coventry which had an air of keeping long-ago secrets, though it was swamped by the city's post-war redevelopment all around.

Yet Ken and Angela weren't cowards, or even timid. They confronted their present cheerfully enough, were mostly quite happy in it and not naïve about its advantages. Angela was a feminist, grateful to be liberated from the tyranny of pleasing; Ken was a socialist, so couldn't regret the end of feudalism or the aristocracy. He even, in the abstract, hoped for a better future, though in truth he was afraid that the best days of socialism were behind them, and its best minds. Of necessity, because of his work at the library, he was an early adopter of new information technologies, though he regretted their consequences in the wider society: he was involved in setting up Early English Books Online. Slim and compact and not unhandsome in his dark suit, he was small—by the time Cecilia was thirteen both his women were taller—with a neatly trimmed beard and brown eyes that were unexpectedly liquid and expressive, suggesting he held back strong feeling. His speech was constrained and quick, and at the library he was respected and even feared, passionate in support of his ideas, contemptuous of interference. He might have lived entirely sufficient to himself, if he hadn't once, on an improbable occasion—he didn't as a rule attend evening receptions at work—encountered Angela with her startled look and panicky laugh. She had said something original and not stupid about the Tudor mentality.

Angela could have been very pretty if she hadn't so determinedly refused that cup, willing it to pass from her. She was fine-boned and dainty, with a translucent complexion—if she looked in a mirror, though, she avoided her own eyes. Her pale silky hair, cut short, seemed to lift in a perpetual breeze of static; searching as she worked on her writing for the right sentence, or the detail of a scene, she combed her fingers through it unconsciously until it crackled and stood on end. She didn't wear any make-up or perfume. Her own mother, Cecilia's grandmother, who was elegant and drank and had lovers, had remonstrated when Angela was younger: if only she'd move more gracefully, less jerkily, if only she'd try contact lenses and wear dresses instead of shirts and slacks and flat shoes. Angela had advanced unhappily towards her middle age, when surely such pressures must come to an end. And then before she was forty, when she was on her third book—her second had been a minor hit—and just around the time that she met Ken, her mother died, and so never knew that her awkward daughter had succeeded in hooking a man after all. Weeping angry tears,

Angela allowed herself this bitterness after the funeral, mock-ing her mother and herself—but only when she was alone, in her most private thoughts.

IT WAS AS IF, ON THE FIRST MORNING OF THAT HOLIDAY IN Florence, Cecilia simply woke up inside the wrong skin. She was on a pull-out bed in her parents' hotel room—they couldn't have afforded a separate room even if it had crossed their minds that she needed it. When she opened her eyes she hardly knew where she was at first, only saw the bright bar of sunlight slanting across the shadows from the window whose blind fitted imperfectly, and felt its alien heat press on her limbs. She'd kicked the sheet down to her feet during the night, and her nightdress had snaked up under her arms and was wrapped around her like a twisted rope, as if in her sleep she'd tried to drag it off. Really, the bed was too nar-row for her and too short. It was a modest hotel, so it didn't have air conditioning, although it was clean; they had stayed there before, and at home in England they referred jocularly to Signora Petricci, the proprietress, as if she were an old friend. Actually that was Cecilia's first coherent thought as she came to consciousness, even before she opened her eyes: that when they had spoken with the Signora last night on arrival she had not, after all, been the creature of their fond recollection, their possession. She had been perfectly polite and smiling, she'd said she remembered them. But hadn't Cecilia caught, while her father unzipped pockets inside his bag, retrieving the passports and a printout of their reservation one by one from where they'd been meticulously stowed, a momentary flash on the Signora's face—vivid and brooding, like the faces on Coptic sarcophagi—of suppressed impatience, or disdain? Or worse, indifference. She did not really like them, she didn't even dislike them. It was as if Cecilia had heard distinctly, in a moment when no one was actually speaking, Signora Petricci's idle thought: *Fussy little man.*

And although Cecilia's Italian was limited, and she certainly didn't know the word for *fussy,* she had seemed nonetheless to hear the thought in Italian and not English—with all Italian's eloquence, its assertive pleasure in its own music and its rhetorical flourish, sublimely confident of its way. It had never fully occurred to Cecilia before, though of course she had known it rationally, that the lives of the people they encountered on holiday must continue here for all the rest of the year while they were absent: as hoteliers and waiters, as men and women. Last night in the restaurant the waitress had slammed down their plates of pasta on the table so hard that they had exchanged surreptitious smiles; now Cecilia remembered the shameless curve of that waitress's haunches in her tight short skirt, her face coarse with make-up—eyeliner and thick green eyeshadow—and felt afraid of her. When they were at home in England, planning their trip, everything in Italy had seemed to belong to them, as if it were their refuge. Now that they had arrived she understood that abroad was not really safe, in the way a museum was safe. Yet they'd been abroad so often: they saved every year for their trips to Italy and France and Greece, and Cecilia had never been afraid of it before.

No doubt she could easily be rid of this fear, she thought.

There would be a trick to it. She just needed a different way of looking at what she seemed to have seen. For reassurance she glanced at her parents' sleeping forms in the bed at whose foot her own little truckle was made up, but they were only mounds under the white sheet, their stillness for the moment too monumental to disturb. In any case she hardly knew what question to ask, whose answer could put her mind at rest. Pulling her nightdress down, making herself decent, she turned on her side to try to sleep again. The sleeve of her mother's checked cotton shirt intruded into her awareness, dangling beside her pillow where Angela had hung it the night before, over the back of a chair where the early sunlight caught it. This shirt was so intensely familiar: soft with washing, sweet with the smell of her mother's soap, innocent, derided—because Cecilia and her father weren't above sometimes teasing Angela about her indifference to what she wore. Cecilia seemed to have a memory from early childhood of sleeping with it pressed against her face for comfort, although that surely wasn't the same shirt. In the beam of hard new light, however, she was ashamed of it. The cloth was faded and blurred, and the frayed cuff sprouted a fringe of broken threads where the interlining showed through.

She remembered how yesterday, when Signora Petricci had laid out on the reception desk the necessary forms for signing, her lace-trimmed cuff had been impeccably laundered and pressed, brilliantly white against her dark skin; links in a gold chain had stirred and glinted with her wrist's authoritative crisp movement, in a way that seemed to have some meaning for Cecilia, send some message. The Signora's cuff and her bracelet were breaches in the fortress of familiarity, through which doubt flooded.

SHE HAD HOPED THAT BREAKFAST WOULD DISPEL THESE TROU-bles. Her mother loved the breakfasts at the Hotel Salvia and said they were "the real thing," which all the hotels had served when she came to Florence as a girl: a jug of coffee and a big-ger jug of hot milk, fresh rolls and white unsalted butter, noth-ing much else. The little dining room spilled into a courtyard where oleander and bougainvillea grew in terracotta pots, and tables were set out under a striped awning. Boldly Angela ordered in Italian, smiling and gesturing with her hands more than she did at home: not tea, no thank you, yes they were English but they wanted coffee, they loved the coffee here— and hot chocolate for their daughter. Ken spread out his guide-book and map on the table and began planning their day; he was annoyed there was no signal for his smartphone, and the hotel Wi-Fi didn't seem to work in the courtyard.

Everything wasn't all right though. Cecilia's unease per-sisted, she writhed with consciousness. There was something wrong with her top, and with her trousers, they didn't fit, or they didn't look right. The Italian girls at the next table, about her own age or younger, looked right: with their Lycra shorts and white crop-tops, their dancing bare midriffs so flat and brown, veils of shining hair flying behind them as they turned. Cecilia had liked her own clothes when she packed them, but overnight they had transformed into a torment, their wrong-ness burning against her skin—which wasn't flawlessly golden.

Because it wasn't just her clothes, it was also her body inside them. She had understood before, when she looked at certain girls at school—even certain scowling ones, who hated lessons, and slouched in their uniforms with half the buttons undone, and spent their lunch break swooning over their phones—that she wasn't beautiful. But there had seemed then to be something unassailable in her, balanced against her lack and compensating for it. If they were beautiful, at least she was the one who *saw* it, saw everything. That had set her apart. Now, on this awful morning in Italy, seeing things and knowing them seemed an inadequate defence. Those girls at the next table were silly, but they were worldly, she thought, trying out that word. They were in the world, and she and her parents were somehow shut out of it. When she dipped buttered roll into her hot chocolate it dripped onto her top, which was the last straw; blinking resentful tears, she pushed away the cup. Her parents picked up on her mood, exchanging concerned glances. Everything was ruined, she exclaimed. Angela reassured her that the top didn't matter, they could soak it.

BUT EVERYTHING WAS RUINED. IN THE STREETS THAT DAY, AND on all the subsequent days of their week's holiday, Cecilia suffered because she felt sure that they weren't welcome in Florence. She seemed to intercept glances of open hostility, as stinging as actual lashes across her flesh, so that walking she flinched and hunched her shoulders, though she knew this wasn't attractive. Or she was aware of a disdain that refused even to see them, as if they were only absences cut out against the streets' thick air—so pungent with garlic, meat, wine, car exhaust, an undertow of rot from the river. Her father had explained how Italians had come to resent the tourism which ate at the physical and social fabric of their cities, but she hadn't really imagined, and perhaps he hadn't either, that this opprobrium was meant for them. It was meant for the other tourists, surely: the ones who left litter and drank beer in the street, or snaked numbly without enthusiasm after the ignorant guides holding their flags or umbrellas aloft. The ones who didn't appreciate what they were seeing. And yet she wondered now how the Florentines were supposed to distinguish, among the hordes wandering up and down. Didn't a discriminating tourist look much like an undiscriminating one?

On Wednesday, when they'd finally gained entrance to the Uffizi Gallery, after an hour or so of waiting in the queue for ticket holders, and then more unzipping in her father's bag, and quarrelling over printouts of his bookings, and his extreme exasperation with the inefficient system—so that Angela had to take over, flustered, appeasing and apologising—Cecilia saw the paintings they'd anticipated so eagerly with a kind of horror. Yet she'd visited the gallery at least twice before on previous holidays, and was supposed to love it. She was so interested in art history, her parents always said; she'd been quick, even when she was quite little, to pick up on the logic of the changes between different periods, the evolution of realism in perspective. In the past, she thought now, there must have been some veil between her eyes and these paintings, so that she could look at them unharmed, without actually taking in their stories. Today that veil was ripped away. There was so much nakedness, to begin with—bodies stripped naked for torture and crucifixion, or for torturous pleasures. A scaly demon was tethered on a chain like a pet. There was such flaunting wealth and beauty, such exotic improbable belief and such ostentatious performances of piety, such cruelty, such laying on of gold. Abraham held down his own son's head with a practised hand, ready with the knife for his neck, and in the son's face was his whole dreadful knowledge of the world. Cecilia looked quickly at her parents, to see if they saw in the Caravaggio what she did. But Angela was enraptured, with pink cheeks; Ken stared at it obstinately, only pretending to be absorbed. He was refusing to move aside for a Spanish boy in shorts, who wanted a photo of his girlfriend standing in front of it.

ON THEIR LAST DAY, LATE IN THE AFTERNOON, THEY WENT TO San Miniato al Monte. It was a long walk in the heat up a winding road, and they went the wrong way for a while. Yet when they arrived at the church at last, Cecilia was almost able to enjoy it. Her relief because their holiday was almost over seemed to mingle with the lightness and grace of the temple-like white facade, perched airily high above the sweltering city and its sluggish shallow river, where on their way up they'd watched a heron fishing, up to its knees in the green water, among the weeds and washed-up heaps of plant debris. On the hill a breeze stirred the tall cypresses; swallows darted, shrilling, in the great bowl of light below them. Warily, almost grudgingly, something unfurled in her which had been tightly compressed, and she allowed herself to know that the place was lovely. It was lovely if you knew how to open yourself to it, take it inside. She felt herself breathing freely for the first time in days.

Her parents were grateful for this reprieve. They, too, were smiling, relaxing into the moment; Cecilia knew that she had spoiled the holiday for them, with her mute rebellion. She hadn't protested explicitly, or made any actual scenes apart from the one at breakfast over the hot chocolate, but the muscles of her face had seemed set hard in their heavy sulk even if she tried to smile, and she'd moved everywhere as reluctantly as if her limbs were made of wood. If her parents spoke to her she could only reply curtly, in monosyllables. Ken and Angela had kept up a bright appearance of enjoying themselves, but it was threadbare, and the strain had told: they had quarrelled more tensely than usual over directions and plans. Their quarrels weren't tempestuous, only dry remarks and things not said. Once or twice in the evenings Angela had put a hand on her daughter's forehead as if she were ill; Cecilia had shaken her off, frowning. But now she was moved by this sudden thawing of her mood to put an arm around her mother's shoulders. —This has always been my *favourite* place, Angela eagerly concurred with her.

They moved inside the church, submerging in a cool dimness that was like a bath for the spirit, and as their eyes adjusted they took in its high solidity, supported on mighty pillars; underfoot, the black and white marble floor was patterned with symbols. The place was busy with tourists, as well as with worshippers arriving for vespers. The three of them went around together as they had in the old days, commenting in subdued voices; Ken read aloud to them from the guidebook, Angela noticed oddities and quirky characters in the margins of the pictures and carvings. A blade of brilliant light struck across the mysterious darkness, as the sun declined behind the high windows. It made the gold mosaics gleam, and caught the jewels in the haloes of gigantic figures arrayed in their glory in the curve of the dome: Christ and the Virgin and San Miniato, who had apparently picked up his own head and carried it here after his martyrdom. Cecilia felt that she, too, was ready for something extraordinary. And at the appointed hour, just as their guidebook had promised, the transfiguring music of plainsong rose from the crypt below them, a few wide steps down from the main body of the church.

Angela pointed out that, now the service had begun, they weren't supposed to go down these steps, but Ken insisted—he wasn't going to miss the Spinello Aretino frescoes in the sacristy. As they descended past the crypt, looking respectfully away from the congregation and choir at their worship, an ancient monk in a white robe, bent and leaning on a stick, hobbled over to block their path. Striking and exaggerated as a work of art, he could have stepped out of one of the paintings they'd been admiring. His bald skull was polished a deep yellow-brown and spotted with age; when he accosted them his loose old lips were stretched in a wide smile, but it wasn't kind, and his eyes glinted with rage in their shadowy sockets. He seemed like fate, or doom, to Cecilia. *Che fate voi qui?* His sing-song speech wasn't personal, it was like the chanted responses, an incantation passed down through the centuries.

Ken pretended not to know what he meant, or perhaps really hadn't understood; he smiled blankly at the monk and continued down into the sacristy. Angela tried to say something in Italian about how much they loved the church, but the old man fastened his gaze on Cecilia, as if he knew she was the most guilty, or the most susceptible. She had no defences, no layers of justification or self-possession, and quailed under his scourging, remorseless look.

What *were* they doing here? His smile was full of knowledge of them and their type. Cecilia hated the old man, but felt in the churning of her adolescent shyness that he was right: this was his place, not theirs. Their poking over the church, with their puny interest in art, was obscene. She appealed to her mother, pulling at her arm. She had period pains, she said. She wasn't feeling well and wanted to go back to the hotel—could Angela please give her the key card for their room? Angela was dismayed: was she sure she knew the way back? Of course she knew it, Cecilia said, glowering. She wasn't an idiot.

ANGELA HATED THE IDEA OF HER FLEEING ALONE THROUGH the city, and wanted to go after her, but Ken said that would only make things worse. He was severe, as if even Cecilia had finally crossed some line beyond which there was only implacable judgement. They would have to get used to this sort of thing now she was a teenager, he said in a tone full of foreboding.

And Angela knew that he was probably right. Cecilia wanted to be alone. If she made an effort she could imagine her daughter hurrying through the crowd in the streets, as clearly as if she were clairvoyant; writing her novels was like clairvoyance sometimes, and involved this same intense sympathy, alongside insights that were more ruthless. Cecilia's fists were clenched at her sides, her head was down, she was hot and she strode clumsily, planting her feet as if she hated herself—though her anxiety was subsiding as she got closer to the familiar terrain around their hotel, and farther away from her parents and their burdens of expectation, their oppressive familiarity. Unexpectedly Angela found herself thinking, in a spirit of protecting Cecilia from all the dangers out there: Move more gracefully, less jerkily. Look up, don't hunch your shoulders.

She imagined her arriving back at the hotel, getting past the reception desk and letting herself into the room, the sheer blissful relief of it, alone at last, with the beds made neatly and the shutters closed on the semi-darkness inside. She would flop down on the bed—their bed, not hers—and feel herself seeping back gradually inside her own shape, belonging to herself alone. But she wouldn't fall asleep, and after a while when she was rested she'd begin to prowl around the room, snooping idly, the way girls do, through her mother's toiletries and in the chest of drawers where they'd unpacked their clothes. And then Angela remembered for no reason a lipstick she'd picked up from her mother's dressing table after she died, when they'd been sorting out the house. She had kept it in a pocket of her handbag for years, though she didn't know why—she never wore lipstick herself, and this one was nothing special, its ridged gold case scratched and grubby, the orange colour inside worn to a nub. Its cloying cakey perfume had reminded her of her mother, she supposed, though she'd only taken it out once or twice to sniff it. When she was a little girl she'd been enchanted by twisting the cylinder, winding the pillar of lipstick up and down. After a while she'd forgotten it was in her handbag, though sometimes accidentally, searching for keys or an aspirin, she'd touched its cool, inert shape in the bag's depths, meaningful and sombre like a bullet. Anyway, she didn't have it now, it had been left behind somewhere.

Angela was remembering all this, and feeling such a strong surge of sorrowful loss, and at the same time she was studying with interest the miraculous rescue of St. Placidus from drowning, painted on the wall in the sacristy of San Miniato. St. Placidus was rolling fatalistically amid the blue waves of his pond, while one of his comrades, endowed with special powers by St. Benedict, came walking across the water to save him. In the picture it looked like such a harmless little pond, carved into the earth as neatly as a stamped-out circle of pastry, or a hole cut into ice for fishing.

Old Friends

—WE HAVE TO WAIT, SALLY SAID, AND CHRISTOPHER TOOK IT
from her because that was his nature: not malleable, but subtly
attentive to other people's necessities and prohibitions. Perhaps
another man would have insisted on his moment in the sun of
their passion, would have seized her and carried her off, but
he was not another man. Anyway, any carrying-off scenario
was bound to be messy, had to include the complication of
the children, her children and Frank's—two boys and a girl,
all handsome and characterful and opinionated, all with their
mother's distinctive auburn hair. The older two were taller
already than Sally and rather too prone, or so Christopher
thought, to bossing her about. Not that she was a pushover:
although she was as small and slight as a girl she was resilient
and forceful. Other people thought Sally a sweet bland competent good woman, the perfect counterpart to Frank's noise
and bluster and the whole exaggerated scale of Frank's personal
operation, which drew in everyone else like a baggage train
dragged after some showy emperor (he was a war correspon-

dent for the BBC). Christopher, however, knew Frank's wife's quick, fierce look, her private judgement. Naturally she adored her children and thought them marvellous, which he didn't quite, so that he saw with clearer eyes than hers how she fell, in her relation to them, into a performance of deploring and forgiving and being put upon, and how the older two were hardening, as their glossy beauty ripened, into a sense of their entitlement to this. They were also Frank's children, after all.

So although Christopher and Sally loved each other, and although he believed they were perfectly suited—eager and diffident, serious, she fitted into the shape of his own serious nature like a nut in its nutshell—they would have to wait, just as if they were characters in an old story. He wasn't sure what they were waiting for, he didn't ask, he didn't want to press her in this place where all the difficulty, it painfully appeared to him, was hers. With women he had always been shy: legacy no doubt of the ghastly school he and Frank had attended together, though it didn't seem to have inhibited Frank. In his working life Christopher was boldly imaginative; against the grain of a family tradition which favoured PPE and the Foreign Office, he'd become an engineer with his own medium-sized business, manufacturing turbines for renewables. But he had found himself in an unknown, dreadful territory, falling in love with the wife of his old friend. All the falling in love he'd ever done before (he'd even been married for a few years, unsuit-ably but amiably enough, when he was very young) had been child's play compared with the power, and the complication, of this.

If he hadn't known what he knew about Frank, and in fact

if Sally hadn't confided in him, appealed to him, made the first move, he'd never have dreamed of doing anything but admiring her chivalrously from a safe distance, and thinking that she was wasted on his friend. But now he was involved, committed up to his neck—over his head in fact: submerged in her astonishingly. So he had to trust that Sally knew what they must do next, or not do. He waited. And in the meantime they snatched what encounters they could, an afternoon here and there at his flat in town; it could never be often enough, and they had never, at least after their beginning, spent a whole evening alone together, not to speak of a night. He had a business to run, Sally had a family, and she also managed to do something or other part-time for the British Council (which was her cover story, too, when she came to him and left her mother, never undomesticated Frank, holding the fort at home).

Christopher's West Hampstead flat was so transformed by her visits that he could hardly recognise his old convenient refuge, and was uneasy spending time in there without her, preferring to drive back at night even when it was late to the anonymous box of a place he rented near his factory, in Gloucestershire. Certain indelible images seemed to be projected like home movies against that London flat's white walls: which were too vacantly receptive because he'd never got round to decorating and hanging up pictures as he ought to. Sally said she loved his flat, the emptiness of it, the unfilled blank spaces—they made her feel free. All the surfaces in her own life, she said, were written over and over in every direction, like an old letter.

.   .   .

THE THING HAD BEGUN ON ONE AFTERNOON OF DRAMA WHEN Christopher had arrived for a visit at Frank and Sally's house outside Southwold on a hot Sunday in summer. It was an old crumbling low stone farmhouse with deep-set windows, smothered on the side facing the road in a silver-limbed hoary ancient rambler whose roses burned intensely red in the strong light; but Sally said the garden was too much work and that she was often lonely here, would rather have lived in the city. How typical of Frank to cherish an ideal of a home in a lovely country place where he could charm and entertain, like the model of an English rural romantic, flowing over with his own bounteous hospitality—and then to abandon his wife and children in it for months at a time while he was away working. On this occasion too Frank was going off somewhere, and he'd asked Christopher to come over to say goodbye, "keep Sally's spirits up" after his departure.

They had all been out in the back garden when Christopher arrived, and the low rooms indoors, fragrant from the meat roasting with garlic in the kitchen, were dim and cool and restful; he could hear the children shrieking and splashing in the pool. Stepping into the glare again, through the French windows at the back of the house onto the sloping lawn, he seemed to catch the married couple just for one instant as they were when he wasn't present—seated tense with concentration on their canvas folding chairs, on the terrace Frank had energetically built one past summer, jingling the ice in their gin-and-tonics, intimately unspeaking, in the middle of something. For once Sally's lifted sharp vixen-face—for that was how he had thought about it since that day, now that he loved her: the velvety fine fur of her skin, russet colouring, slanting long muzzle-like lines of her cheekbones—had been unsmiling and naked, with no charming or placatory mask fixed in its place.

Then Frank had jumped up at the sight of Christopher: relieved, Christopher thought, by their being interrupted, as if that were exactly what he'd been invited for. Dropping a heavy hot arm across his friend's shoulders, Frank hailed him exuberantly; Christopher felt overdressed because Frank was only wearing khaki cargo shorts and flip-flops. His big brown belly shoved round and tight and unapologetic above his shorts like a pregnant woman's, and there were forceful scrabbles of black hair on his plump breasts and on his toes; he was one of those men who thrust his imperfect body shamelessly, even keenly, in your line of sight, with a winning, childlike, unin-hibited unconsciousness, as if he'd never noticed he wasn't a cherub any longer. Christopher in his late forties was still straight and slim, six inches taller than Frank and with more hair, even if its fair colour had bleached to neutral; he was pleasant-looking, with a long face, chalky complexion, pale blue eyes. And yet somehow it was ugly Frank, with his sag-ging baby-face and the untidy bald circle in his black curls, who took everyone's attention, the women watching him and enjoying him, and some of the men. They succumbed to his energy, and his self-love.

As soon as Christopher had arrived Frank was in his ele-ment, talking, talking; walking up and down the garden with some new flame-throwing gadget he'd acquired to kill weeds in the lawn, blasting at them perilously and leaving black-ened patches, talking all the while in his loud, eager, confiding voice, punctuated with shouts of laughter: politics mostly, and gossip about personalities, and books—not fiction (only Sally, of the three of them, read fiction). It was their tradition that Christopher countered Frank with his quiet irony, his good information. He was the corrective to Frank's dogmatism, his quick-fix partisanship; it was to Frank's credit that he sought out his friend's dissent. The oldest boy, Nicholas, had come out of the pool after a while, wrapped in a towel and shivering with wet hair, drawn helplessly to follow the flame-thrower. After lunch—Frank had carved, wielded the knife in alarming proximity to his own naked belly, although Sally remonstrated with him mildly, asked him to put his shirt on, pointed out that she'd made the children get dressed decently before they were allowed at the table—Christopher helped Sally to clear the plates while Frank went to pack, hardly able to repress his jubilation at his imminent escape. —It's all right for you lucky blighters, he yelled downstairs. —Living the life down here in the country idyll. Some of us have to get back to work, do a reality check!

And then something happened in the pool: a change in the noise of the children's idling, a splash, and awful screams brought the adults running down from the house. But all three children seemed to be okay at first, quarrelling and shoving at the pool's edge, streaming with wet, accusing one another. —Corin's such an idiot! Nicholas was shouting. —Showing off as usual. Why can't he do anything properly? He's got no sense.

The younger boy began staggering about and pretending to puke, or half-puking, in what looked like a pantomime performance of drunkenness. —Is he putting it on? Sally asked, bemused.

—Really he was floating right on the bottom, Mum, Amber said. —It was his own fault. Nicky and me had to dive down to get him out.

—Don't fuck about though, Frank said to his children genially enough. —This is serious stuff. You're all right, aren't you?

When the little one dropped abruptly to his knees, still retching and choking, his eyes rolling up into his head, it was Christopher who scooped him quickly up and performed the necessary manoeuvres, laying him flat on his stomach on the grass and turning his head, making sure he didn't swallow his tongue, then pumping his frail shoulder blades so that he vomited up quite a quantity of pool-water, mixed with lunch. —My God, my God, Sally whispered in panic and sympathetic horror, crouching beside them, hardly daring in that moment to touch her own child, covering up her mouth with both her hands.

—But he's all right, isn't he? said Frank. —I mean, you can't get out of a pool and walk around and still be drowning, can you?

Once Corin was sitting up again and swearing, weeping, hiding his messy face against Sally and side-swiping with a fist at his brother, Christopher agreed that everything was probably fine now, but said they still ought to take him to a hospital for checking out. Frank was visibly torn—he had a plane to catch. —You go to the airport, Christopher said. —It's only a routine, make sure the lungs are clear. I don't mind.

And so it was that he had spent all that afternoon and evening waiting in Southwold and District with Sally and Corin; Frank had dropped off the other two children, on his way out, to sleep over at a friend's house. Eventually the doctors cleared them to go home. Christopher carried the sleeping child through the front garden from the car in the moonlight, and laid him in his bed while Sally pulled up the duvet tenderly to cover him; Christopher felt as if he'd trespassed for a moment inside the heart of a family life, which was something he'd always wanted for himself but not contrived to get. —You must be flat out, you poor thing, he said sympathetically to Sally once they'd closed the bedroom door behind them. —Can I get you a nightcap? Or would you like tea? Would you like me to stay?

He had truly only meant that he could kip down, if she liked, in a spare room: make quite sure that she and Corin were both all right in the morning. But the moment the words were out of his mouth he understood how they could be interpreted as a commitment to more than merely friendliness; and Sally had turned to him, there in the dim light on the landing, burying her face in his shirt front with a sob of self-abandonment, clinging to him, dropping her whole weight—which wasn't very much—against him. —I would like you to stay, I would, she said. Of course it was partly the strain of her afternoon. —He didn't even ring, did he? To find out how Corin was.

I left my phone on deliberately, the whole time, even though you're not supposed to in the hospital.

Christopher tightened his grip cautiously around her, taking her weight. —Of course I can see, he said, —that old Frank could be quite a trial, to be married to.

—Oh, Chris, she groaned, —you don't know the half of it.

Later in bed—they hadn't quite wanted to make love that first time, not in the same house as the sleeping child saved from disaster, as if that might be unlucky; so that Sally had stayed underneath the duvet and he had stayed on top of it, and the duvet had functioned as a bolster between them, while Christopher held her in his arms to comfort her—she told him quite a lot about the half of it he didn't know. Although perhaps he knew, or could have guessed, somewhat more of it than he let on: that it wasn't only women Frank was unfaithful with, and that some of the boys he had when he was abroad were kids, they were really only kids, only just past the age of consent, and that he refused to get himself tested for anything, and that when he woke up with nightmares he needed Sally to comfort him like a baby. And that he'd never ever even once, not once, it was a joke, been there for any of the children's concerts or birthdays or parent evenings, even though he'd made such a huge deal out of sending them to all those private schools which they couldn't really conceivably afford. Because naturally there were chronic problems with money too. And as for his drinking, don't get her started on that. Frank's eternal absences, Sally said, were the least of her worries. They were the good bit.

· · ·

AND THEN, WHEN CHRISTOPHER AND SALLY HAD BEEN LOVING each other clandestinely for about eighteen months, Frank died reporting on the war in Syria: which you might have thought, looking at it cynically, must be the sort of thing they had been waiting for. It wasn't a heroic death, he wasn't shot or blown up or anything, though he might have been, he'd always pushed forward fearlessly into the worst places, despite his nightmares and his secret fears. But he got blood poisoning through a cut in his foot and died remarkably quickly, before anyone even really knew that anything was wrong, in some chaotic hospital on the Turkish border which had been turned upside-down by the war and had no antibiotics.

Christopher heard the news from a friend of a friend who rang him at his office in town. The strangest thing was that he'd already caught sight of Sally and the children that very same morning, before he got the call, just for a few seconds, quite by the most improbable chance—because in London who ever accidentally crossed paths with anyone they knew? He'd been on foot, on his way to a meeting, when he saw Sally driving down Euston Road with all the children, tensely concentrated at the wheel of Frank's preposterous SUV, which was splattered in Suffolk mud. He knew she hated driving in London, and after they'd gone past he'd even wondered, because there was no possible reason for them to all be there on a school-day morning, whether he might have conjured them up out of his desire for Sally, like his hallucinations of her presence in his flat.

Something in the collection of their solemn, striking faces—beautifully alike as a donor's family lined up in graduated profile in a Renaissance altarpiece, all blue-white skin and rusty silky hair, gazing alertly forwards through the windscreen at the traffic—had troubled him even at the time. Lifted in the SUV up above the ordinary level of the street, they had seemed so inaccessible to him. He understood, as soon as he heard the news about Frank, that their bereavement had already fallen onto them, like a cloak—not of invisibility, but of apartness. He called Sally right away, but she didn't pick up, so he texted. *When can we meet?*

You've heard? she texted back, after a little while.

I've heard.

I'm in town, talking to the FO, she sent. *We have to wait.*

THEY HAD FRANK'S BODY FLOWN HOME AND AT HIS FUNERAL, where of course Christopher was too—in fact he'd more or less organised it, Sally was in pieces—the distinguished, desolated family made a heart-rending picture, which went the rounds of all the media. You could hardly tell, until you looked carefully, that tiny Sally wasn't a fourth orphaned child. And after the funeral Christopher was often in their Southwold home for days and weeks at a time, helping Sally out, going through Frank's papers and his clothes with her, though she wasn't good at throwing things away, sorting out probate and closing bank accounts, getting the house ready to put it in the hands of the estate agents. He always slept in the spare room. Once he tried to embrace her when the children were all away, Nicholas boarding at school now (it was what he wanted, and Christopher paid) and the other two at sleepovers. —I can't,

Sally said apologetically, shaking her head, pushing her palms against his chest, not meeting his eyes. —Not here. Not yet.

When a year had passed they began talking about buying a house together; Sally had said she hated the country but now it seemed she didn't want to move into London after all, so he looked in Gloucestershire and found the perfect place. But she still wasn't ready. —I don't know what to tell the kids, she said. —Not so soon, when they're still grieving for their father.

Christopher wondered how much the children were really grieving. They had been shocked out of their serenity and complacency, certainly; sometimes they were self-important with their loss, used it as leverage in their quarrels with Sally. But actually he thought they didn't miss their father hugely, as if they hadn't known him very well. They probably didn't miss him as much as Christopher did—he felt Frank's absence every day: the space in life where his friend's noise and his bullying exuberance were missing, and his warmth, and the waste of his death. The children didn't mind Christopher. Amber aged twelve in her cropped top, wound around with beads and painted with Sally's eyeshadow and lipstick, flashed her flawless prepubertal midriff at him. —Why don't you just sleep with my mother, Christopher, she drawled, —if you're so mad about her?

—Well, I am mad about her, he said, blushing. —But it's not quite as easy as all that.

CHRISTOPHER INSISTED EVENTUALLY—FOR THE SAKE OF HIS own dignity, really, and his self-possession—that Sally come to talk it all out with him at his flat: which wasn't exactly neutral territory, haunted by the times they had spent there together. The place was still spartan, he hadn't done anything to it or bought any more furniture, hadn't wanted to change anything. When he asked why she wouldn't live with him she sat on the side of his bed with her head in her hands, fox-red hair falling forwards over her face. He dragged over a box of the books he'd never got round to unpacking and sat down on it, opposite to her, close enough to touch but not touching, watching her intently.

—It isn't the children really, is it? he gently said. —It's you.

—Chris, I can't leave the house. Frank's present in it everywhere. I can't leave him. I feel all the things I didn't use to feel. Think of his achievements! I'm reading everything he's written. Isn't it so good? And I'm finding all these souvenirs and photographs, things from his childhood and boyhood, trophies and model airplanes and letters he wrote to his mother from school, all that stuff. I'm thinking about all those places he went in his adult life, sending back his reports—I never properly asked, what was it like there? What was it *really* like? I'm cheated, by his leaving me this way. Because something's still unfinished between us.

—Between us? Christopher pressed her, needing to be sure.

—Between Frank and me.

And he knew that although by this time Sally had dropped her hands from her face and was looking right at him, she couldn't see him. Her vision was all filled up with Frank.

Children at Chess

AS SOON AS HE HEARD NEWS OF THE SERIOUS ILLNESS OF HIS sister, he began to think of her as dead. She was a stout, sane, pleasant woman in her late fifties, only ten months older than he was, with grown children and a newish career as a counsellor; in her first career she had taught in a primary school. He had hardly noticed, even, that she had grown middle-aged: probably she dyed her hair. And she still had that childish very pure complexion, white like kitchen china, with lilac shadows; she darted the same old looks of amused observation. They had been great friends when they were children, lonely and self-sufficient, growing up in a succession of European and African cities because their father moved every two or three years with his job, working for an oil company. Their private language had been a ragbag of French and Dutch and Portuguese, so that no one else could understand their jokes. For a while their parents had rented an old colonial house in Luanda, with palm trees and a baobab in the garden, and maids with brown, bare, dusty feet; the cool floor of a courtyard was chequered with tiles like a chessboard. He had been sent back to England, to go to school, when he was thirteen. Because you're the boy, she'd said—not resentful, but exact. Up to that point there had only been a friendly competition between them over who was cleverest. Both of them were quick with facts and figures, they had tested each other out of their history books. In Paris and The Hague they had each been top of their respective classes.

And because his life at that English school had been anguished, a torment, he hadn't allowed himself to imagine that she might have felt left behind, cheated of something. He had pictured her in Luanda, playing on the courtyard floor in the shade, absorbed in some game of her own invention, using the bizarre hard fruits and seeds from the garden as counters, moving them around on the tiles. When they met in the holidays there was a new distance between them. He hadn't ever told her how he suffered, he had presented to her as to everyone his new dry carapace of manliness, disenchanted and absent.

Now he was in data analytics, twice divorced, without children of his own, with more money than he could spend. He wasn't interested in money, he had given a lot away to his sister's children. At weekends sometimes if he was in England he drove over to have Sunday lunch with her and her husband, Angus: a decent and boring man who worked for one of the big pharmaceuticals. In the age of restless globalisation and smartphones, she and Angus still had gin-and-tonics before lunch in summer, in deckchairs on a wide lawn which was mown, by Angus presumably, in old-fashioned stripes of green and paler green, with delphiniums and hollyhocks in the herbaceous border. She was on Facebook, but only in order to keep in touch with her children, and her one grandchild in America; she served up their roast meat on the green and gold dinner service that had been their mother's, and Angus carved it with a knife worn fine by sharpening, which had no doubt been among their wedding presents. He had allowed himself to be amused by her solidity, the safe solidity of her life and Angus's: now this joke of their solidity turned out to be beside the point. Of course he spoke to her about her illness, said all the requisite hopeful, encouraging things. Her slow smile and the alert play of her expression were still the same: the irony in her silence wounded him. He had been sorry when she took up counselling, because he resented the claim of all the mind-sciences and pseudo-sciences, to speak out of depths which were surely cheapened by explanation. Now his heart was filled with ash and madness. He had reconciled himself years ago to the idea of his own death, but it hadn't occurred to him to imagine his sister's.

He fell asleep one afternoon at his desk at home: which wasn't characteristic, he never slept in the day. He awoke confused—with a dry mouth and his sleeve wet where he had dribbled on it—from a dream in which he and his sister were still children, playing chess together at a round table. Under the table he had seemed to feel as a real pressure, sweetly ordinary and consoling, the unselfconscious unsexual weight of her leg against his, or his against hers; he had smelled the stuffy warmth of her wool dress, inseparable from his own warmth. An off-white ribbon was tied in her hair, and he'd thought in the dream that after all he had only to reach back across such a very short distance in time, to feel in his fingers its puckered grosgrain texture and border of scalloped thread-work, and to pull it undone. He had longed to pull at it. And he'd seemed to know that he would win their game of chess, and that she would not show whether she minded. When he woke up he supposed that she'd have some explanation for his dream in her counselling jargon, dipping down into her knowledge of what was hidden in the daytime, hidden inside him. But it had seemed so real to him, that he felt in his pocket for the tiny red chess piece he'd stolen from her, when she wasn't looking.

The Other One

WHEN HELOISE WAS TWELVE, IN 1986, HER FATHER WAS KILLED in a car crash. But it was a bit more complicated than that. He was supposed to be away in Germany at a sociology conference, only the accident happened in France, and there were two young women in the car with him. One of them was his lover, it turned out in the days and weeks after the crash, and the other one was his lover's friend. He'd never even registered at the conference. Didn't it seem strange, Heloise's mother asked long afterwards, in her creaky, surprised, lightly ironic voice, as if it only touched her curiosity, that the two lovebirds had taken a friend along with them for their tryst in Paris? The lover was also killed; her friend was seriously injured. Heloise's mother, Angie, had found out some of these things when she rushed to be at her husband's bedside in a hospital in France: he had lived on for a few days after the accident, though he never recovered consciousness.

That time was blurred in Heloise's memory now, more than thirty years later. She'd been convinced for a while that she'd accompanied her mother to France; vividly she could picture her father motionless in his hospital bed, his skin yellow-brown against the pillow, his closed eyelids bulging and naked without their rimless round glasses, glossy black beard spread out over the white sheet. But Angie assured her that she was never there. Anyway, Clifford had shaved off his beard by then. —I should have known he was shaving it off for someone, Angie said. —And why would I have taken you with me, darling? You were a little girl, and I didn't know what I was going to find when I got there. I've mostly blocked out my memory of that journey—it was the worst day of my life. I've no idea how I got across London or onto the ferry, though strangely I can remember the grey water in the dock, choppy and frightening. I was frightened. I felt surrounded by monstrosities—I suppose I was worried that his injuries might be monstrous. Once I was actually there and I saw him, I was able to grasp everything. I had time to think. It's a bizarre thing to say, but that hospital was a very peaceful place. It was connected to some sort of religious order—there were cold stone floors and a high vaulted ceiling, nuns. Or at least that's how I remember it. I've forgotten the name of the hospital, so I can't google it to check.

—Did you see her?

—Who?

—Delia, the lover.

—Delia wasn't the lover. She was the other one. The lover was killed instantly, in the accident, when they hit the tree. They took her body away.

Heloise and Angie were sitting drinking wine at Angie's

kitchen table, in the same skinny four-storey Georgian house in Bristol where they'd all lived long ago with Clifford, in the time before the accident: Heloise and her older brother, Toby, and their younger sister, Mair. Angie hadn't even changed the big pine kitchen table since then, although she'd done things to the rest of the kitchen—it was smarter and sleeker now than it used to be, when the fashion was for everything to look home-made and authentic. She and Clifford had bought the table from a dealer in the early days of their marriage; she had stripped off its thick pink paint with Nitromors. And then she'd worked with that dealer for a while, going through country houses with him and keeping his best pieces in her home, to show to customers. She couldn't part with the old table, Angie said; so many friends and family had sat around it over the years. And now she was seventy-two.

HELOISE DIDN'T HAVE HER MOTHER'S GIFT OF LIGHTNESS. Angie was tall and thin, stooped, flossy grey silk mingled in her messy, faded hair. Vague and charming, she had escaped from a posh county family whose only passionate feelings, she said, were for dogs and property. Heloise was stocky, top-heavy with bosom, and serious, with thick, kinked tobacco-brown hair and concentrating eyes; she looked more like her father, whose family had come to the East End of London from Lithuania in the early twentieth century. She didn't think her personality was much like his, though; she wasn't audacious. She had kept an obituary clipped out of an academic journal—Angie said she didn't want it—which expressed shock and sadness at the loss of *an audacious original thinker,* whose book *Rites of Passage in Contemporary Capitalist Societies* was *required reading for radicals.* The obituary didn't mention the problem of the lover. And there were no obituaries in any of the big newspapers; Clifford would have felt slighted by that, if he'd been able to know it— he'd have believed it was part of the conspiracy against him. Probably no one read his book these days.

Sometimes, when Heloise spoke to her therapist, she imagined her father's death slicing through her life like a sword, changing her completely with one blow; at other times she thought that in truth she'd always been like this, reserved and sulky, wary. She knew other children of those brilliant, risky marriages of the nineteen-seventies who were taciturn and full of doubt like her. Her parents had been such an attractive, dynamic couple, so outward-turning; the crowd of their friends dropping in to talk and eat and drink and smoke pot was always on the brink of becoming a party. From the landing on the top floor, where their bedrooms were, or venturing farther down the deep stairwell, Toby and Heloise and Mair, along with strangers' children put to sleep on the spare mattresses, had spied over the banisters on the adults, who were careless of what the children saw: shouted political arguments, weeping, snogging; someone flushing her husband's pills down the lavatory; the husband swinging his fist at her jaw afterwards. Angie danced to Joni Mitchell with her eyes closed, T-shirt off, pink nipples bare and arms reached up over her head, long hands washing over each other absorbedly; Clifford tried to burn five-pound notes in the gas fire, yelling to tell everyone that Angie was frigid, Englishwomen of her class were born with an icebox between their legs. Angie called him a "dirty little Jew," and then lay back on her beanbag, laughing at how absurd they both were.

BUT THAT WAS ALL ANCIENT HISTORY, AND NOW HELOISE WAS in her forties, divorced with two young children, running her own small business from home—finding and booking locations for photo shoots—and making just about enough money to live on and pay her half of the mortgage. When she met a woman called Delia at a dinner party, the name didn't strike her at first, it was just a name. It was a late summer's evening, and dinner began with white wine outdoors in a small, brick-walled garden, its smallness disproportionate to the dauntingly tall back of the terraced house, built on a steep hill in Totterdown; there were espaliered apple trees trained around the garden walls. The guests' intimacy thickened as light faded; birds bustled in the dusk amongst the leaves, a robin spilled over with his song, Venus pierced the clear evening sky. They all said they wouldn't talk politics but did anyway, as if their opinions had been dragged out of them, their outrage too stale to be enjoyable. Was it right or wrong to use the word "fascism" to describe what was happening in the world? Was the future of socialism in localism? Their host, Antony, put out cushions on the stone seats and on the grass, because of the cold coming up from the earth; he poured more wine. Heloise had her hair pinned up, she was wearing her vintage navy crêpe dress.

She liked Delia right away.

Delia was older than the rest of them, with a lined, tanned, big-boned face and alert, frank, open gaze; her dark hair was streaked with grey and cut in a gamine style, fringe falling into her eyes, that made her look Italian, Heloise thought: like an Italian intellectual. Round her neck on a cord hung a striking heavy piece of twisted silver, and as the air grew cooler she wrapped herself in an orange stole, loose-woven in thick wool, throwing one end over her shoulder. Everything Delia did seemed graceful and natural. Heloise was full of admiration, at this point in her own life, for older women who managed to live alone and possess themselves with aplomb; she was learning how to be single again, and didn't want to end up like her mother, volatile and carelessly greedy. Delia was a violinist, it turned out, and taught violin to children, Suzuki-style; this was how she'd got to know Antony, because his younger son came to her classes. She hadn't been to his home before, and said that she liked the neat creative order in his garden; it made her think of a medieval garden in a story. And she was right, Heloise thought. There was something Chaucerian about Antony, in a good way, with his pink cheeks and plump hands, soft shapeless waist, baggy corduroy trousers, tortoiseshell-framed glasses, tousled caramel-coloured hair.

—Delia's like the Pied Piper! he enthused. —At the end of the morning she leads the kids around the community centre in a sort of conga line, playing away on these violins as tiny as toys, past the Keep Fit and French conversation and the Alzheimer's Coffee Morning, all of them bowing away like crazy at Schumann and Haydn. Some of these kids have never heard classical music in their lives before. And yet it all sounds great: it's in tune! Or almost in tune, almost!

Antony and Heloise had been close friends since university. He worked for the city planning department, which was innovative and chronically short-staffed and underfunded. Like her, he was bringing up his children as a single parent; his wife had left him and gone back to Brazil. Heloise had secret hopes of Antony. He wasn't the kind of man she'd ever have chosen when they were young together—too gentle, not dangerous enough—but recently she'd come to see him differently. It was like turning a key in the door of her perception, opening it onto a place that had existed all along. How whole Antony was! How nourishing his company, how sound his judgements! She kept her hopes mostly hidden though, even from herself. She was afraid of spoiling their friendship through any misunderstanding, or a move made too soon.

Delia said that intonation always came first, in the Suzuki method. No matter how simple a piece you're playing, it should sound right from the very beginning. The conversation became animated, because the other guests were parents of young children too, and intensely concerned about the creativity of their offspring. Heloise thought that Delia looked amused, as if she were used to parents thinking their children were prodigies, just because they liked banging away on a piano. Antony wished that his older boy would learn, but he had been diagnosed as on the autistic spectrum, and wasn't good at following directions; Heloise thought that this boy was sometimes just plain naughty, though she didn't say so to Antony. When she suggested that she'd like to bring her own five-year-old daughter, Jemima, along to the classes, Delia told her the time and the venue—there were still a couple of places free. Teaching was a great pleasure, she added. She liked the company of children, and had never had any of her own. Heloise marvelled at how calmly Delia talked about herself, not trailing ragged ends of need or display.

—And what about your own playing? somebody asked her. —Do you still play?

She belonged to a quartet that met twice a week, she said, and played sometimes with another friend who was a pianist; they put on concerts from time to time. —I had hopes of playing as a professional when I was young. I won some competitions and dreamed of being a soloist—it was probably only a dream. But then I was involved in a car accident in France, I damaged my neck and my hands, I was ill for a long time. And that was the end of that.

The light was almost gone from the garden. Antony had slipped inside to serve up the food; he was a good cook, appetising smells were coming from the kitchen. Through the open glass doors Heloise could see yellow lamplight spilling over his books piled up on the coffee table, a folded soft plaid blanket on a sofa, the children's toys put away in their toy box; beyond that, a table set with glasses and coloured napkins, a jug filled with fresh flowers and greenery. —It was such a long time ago, Delia said, laughing to console the others when they exclaimed over her awful loss. —Like I said, I was very young. It was really all very tragic, but don't worry. It happened to me in another life.

· · ·

IT WAS POSSIBLE THAT DELIA'S ACCIDENT HAD NOTHING TO do with Heloise's father. There might have been two accidents in France, two Delias. If it was the same accident, then why hadn't she identified Heloise when they met, or guessed whose daughter she was? Heloise was a pretty unusual name. But then, why would Clifford have mentioned his children's names, to a girl who was only his lover's friend? Perhaps he had met Delia for the first time on that fateful day: probably she'd only come along for the drive, a lift to Paris. Anyway, he wouldn't have been talking about his children to either of those young women. He'd have been pretending, at least to himself, that he wasn't really the father of a family, that he could do anything he dared to do, that he was as young and careless and free as these girls were, his life his own to dispose of. And after the accident, when Delia had endured months and perhaps years of suffering and rehabilitation, and lost her hope of a career as a performer, why would she have wanted to find out anything about the family whose happiness had been ruined along with hers? She'd have wanted everything connected with Clifford to fall behind her into oblivion. Into the lead-grey sea.

Heloise talked all these possibilities through with her therapist; she didn't want to talk to anyone else, not yet. The therapist was wary of her excitement. She asked why it was important for Heloise right now to find a new connection with her father, and suggested a link between the breakdown of her marriage and her feelings of abandonment at the time of her father's death. —What did you do, when this woman told the story of her accident? How did you react?

—Somehow I was all right. I'd drunk a couple of glasses of wine, I was feeling surprisingly mellow—for me, anyway. And then, when I suddenly understood who she was—or might be—I felt as if something clicked into place, and I belonged to her. Or she belonged to me. Everything belonged together. It was probably the wine.

Antony had called them in to eat just as Delia was finishing her story, and Heloise had stood up from her cushion on the stone bench elatedly. She'd almost spoken out then and there—but she'd had more sense, knew that this wasn't the right time to open up anything so momentous, not in company. However well balanced Delia appeared, it would be painful to have her buried history brought back to life. So Heloise had gone inside instead, ahead of the others, and put her arms around Antony, who was standing at the sink lifting a tray of vegetables from the bamboo steamer. Because of the kind of man he was, he wasn't annoyed at her getting in between him and the tricky moment of his serving up the food, but put down the vegetables and hugged her back, enthusiastically.
—Hey, what's this in honour of?
—Oh, I don't know. Just. Such a nice dinner party.

He said that she looked lovely in her vintage dress with the art deco brooch, like a learned Jewess from Minsk or Vilnius in the old days, and Heloise had realised that this was exactly the look she'd been trying for. She put her outfits together, always, with the same effort she might use in dressing a room for a shoot, working towards some idea at the back of her mind, like an old photograph or a painting.

For the rest of the evening she'd been more lively and talk-

ative than usual, conscious of hoarding inside her the extraordinary story of the accident, charged with emotion and dramatic
as an opera. Watching Delia, she'd enjoyed the way she held
her fork, the poised, elegant angle of her wrist and her rather
big tanned hand; how she sat up very straight and listened to
the others with intelligent interest, reserving her own judgement. She did have Mediterranean heritage, as Heloise had
guessed, though it was not Italian but Spanish. Her politics
were quite far left but not doctrinaire, she was well informed
and thoughtful. As she grew older, Heloise decided, she'd like
to carry herself off in Delia's easy style, in clothes made out of
homespun wool or linen, dyed in natural earth colours.

JEMIMA WASN'T A MUSICAL PRODIGY, IT TURNED OUT. BUT SHE
enjoyed the Suzuki classes and for a while, in the first flush of
enthusiasm, carried her tiny violin around with her everywhere
at home, tucked under her chin, bowing out her answers to
Heloise's questions in snatches of "Twinkle, Twinkle" or "The
Happy Farmer" instead of words. And Delia in the different
context of the classes was a revelation: not tolerant and encouraging, as Heloise had imagined her, but crisp and unsmiling,
even stern. Making music was not a game, she conveyed, but
an initiation into a realm of great significance. The children
responded well to this, as if it were a relief that something
for once wasn't all about them. Unconsciously they imitated
Delia's straight back, the flourish of her bowing, that dip of
her head on the first beat of the bar; they were carried outside
themselves in the music's flow. Their parents, too, were intimi-

dated and gratified by Delia's severity. She liked them to stay to watch the class, so that they could look out for good practice at home during the week, and mostly they obediently did stay.

Usually Heloise sat through these sessions with Antony, and towards the end of the class one or other of them would go off to pick up the two older boys—Heloise's Solly and Antony's Max—from their football club. Through the crowded busyness of the rest of her week, Heloise anticipated with pleasure this hour of enforced mute stillness, squeezed up against Antony on the community-centre benches, in the big white characterless room, with its missing ceiling tiles and broken Venetian blinds, feeling his companionable warmth along her flank, buoyed up by the children's music. The room smelled of hot plastic from the lights, and of sweat from the Zumba class that came before Suzuki. Sometimes she and Antony bought lunch together afterwards in the café in the centre, depending on how wound up Max was from football. None of this would have been so straightforward if Antony's ex-wife, Carlota, the boys' mother, hadn't gone back to Brazil. Heloise couldn't help herself feeling a surge of selfish relief when she thought of it; she'd found Carlota abrasive and difficult. When she'd told Antony once that her ex-husband, Richard, had complained that she wasn't spontaneous, Antony confessed in exchange that Carlota had called him an old woman. —Which was kind of surprising, he added, with the modest amount of owlish irony he permitted himself. —Coming from her, as she was supposed to be such a feminist.

Heloise had told Antony years ago, when they first knew each other, about her father's accident; although not about the lover, because that had still been shaming then, private. Angie had always wanted to tell everyone everything, as a twisted, crazy joke: wasn't life just bound to turn out like that! Now Heloise came close, on several occasions, to explaining to Antony her opaque connection, through the accident, with Delia: a connection that might or might not exist. Each time, however, the moment passed; Max threw one of his tantrums, or Jemima spilled her water. And she hadn't said anything, yet, to Delia herself—with every week that she delayed, it grew more difficult to imagine bringing up the subject. The whole story seemed so improbably far-fetched, and even if it had really ever happened, it was a million years ago, in another age. At the Suzuki classes, anyway, Delia was too remote, impersonal; she belonged to everyone, it would have been inappropriate to take her aside and make that special claim on her.

Apparently Antony was having viola lessons with her, one evening a week. Heloise hadn't known that he used to play when he was younger. She wished she had some such privileged way into intimacy with Delia; she was shy in the face of the older woman's authority, her self-sufficiency. Delia was always perfectly friendly, but she would never join them for lunch; she rehearsed with her string quartet, she said, on Saturday afternoons. Heloise suspected that Delia took in too, with some distaste, the mess at their shared table in the café: the chips afloat in spilled water, the older boys high with adrenaline from their game, obnoxiously shouty, eyes glittering and faces hot, hair pasted down with sweat.

· · ·

HELOISE'S BROTHER TOBY WAS OVER FROM LA, WHERE HE worked in the music business; he came to spend a few days in Bristol with their mother. Richard had the children on Saturday night, so Heloise went to have supper with Toby and Angie at the old kitchen table. Toby was like their mother, rangy and tall and thin, with silky greying reddish curls; he had the same raw-boned sex appeal that Angie used to have—indolent, indifferent to what anyone thought about him, scratching carelessly at the hollow white belly exposed under his too-short T-shirt, leaning back in his chair and stretching long legs under the table, so that his big feet in scruffy Converse intruded into Heloise's space. He and Angie were mesmerising when they exerted their allure, auburn like angels; and then sometimes they were unabashedly ugly, ill-tempered with their pale-lard colouring, blue eyes small with exhaustion, sex-light withdrawn like a favour they were bored with proffering.

Angie was happy because Toby was there; she was girlish and clowning. In honour of the occasion she'd made something ambitious for supper, quesadillas which had to be assembled at the last minute—and then Toby mixed LA-style martinis which she said made her too drunk to cook safely. He had to griddle the enchiladas, with a lot of smoke and noise, under her laughing supervision, as she hung onto his shoulder. Heloise thought that her mother, despite her fierce feminism, actually preferred the company of men, powerful men. Women's winding approaches to one another, all the encouraging and propitiating, made her impatient; she'd rather be up against men's bullishness, their frank antagonism—she had even enjoyed sparring with Richard. And Angie liked

Toby's making fun of her radicalism, as if she were a Trotskyite firebrand extremist, while she accused him of selling out; they had this teasing, challenging rapport. Still, it was notable that he'd chosen to live thousands of miles away from her.

Heloise had thought that she might speak to them about Delia. Perhaps her mother could tell her something which would make it clear at least whether this was the right Delia. But she was surprised, once she was inside her old home, by her reluctance to mention her new discovery. She could imagine Angie taking Delia up, inviting her round to talk, celebrating her, the pair of them growing close, bound together by their long-ago disaster. Or Angie might be scathing, and recoil from making any new connection with those days. So when Heloise told them about Jemima's Suzuki class, she didn't mention the teacher's name. Angie loved the idea of Jemima communicating through her violin. She was an inspired, enthusiastic grandmother, throwing herself into her grandchildren's world, siding with them and seeing everything at their eye level; also fretting to Heloise and Mair, when Toby wasn't there, about the teenage son he had in the US and never saw, from a marriage that hadn't lasted a year. Mair complained that Angie had reinvented herself over the decades. —You'd think now that she was some hippie earth-mother, dedicated to her offspring. Which isn't exactly the childhood I remember.

Inevitably they talked about politics in America; Toby knew a lot, in his laconic, disparaging way. Watching out for totalitarianism, they said, everyone had been oblivious to the advent of the illiberal democracies. And what did it mean for the world, if America's compass was no longer set to liberal?

But it had never really been set there in the first place, Angie protested. Toby played them his latest music, then went hunting upstairs in a cupboard for a box of cassette tapes from his youth, came down with a quiz game and a cricket bat. He tried to make them play the game, but too many questions referred to TV stars and football contests they'd forgotten—in fact, to a whole vanished world of perception. Heloise told awful stories about Richard; there was such relief in not having to defend him to her family any longer. By eleven o'clock Angie was drained, done for. This was something she had to get used to, she said, now that she was an old woman. Weariness came rattling down all at once in her mind, like a metal shutter across a window, peremptory and imperative, so that she had to go to bed. —But I wish that you'd really begin to be an old woman! Heloise joked, placating her. —It's about time. Shouldn't you be knitting? You're meant to be tedious and repetitive by now. With a nice perm.

—Toby thinks I'm tedious and repetitive already.

Angie couldn't help flirting with her son, wanting his reassurance. Cruelly Toby smiled back at her, implacable. And she did look old at that moment, under the bright kitchen light, despite her lovely careless dress with its zigzag print: loose skin on her face was papery, her shoulders were stooped, her skull shone through her thinning hair. Heloise couldn't help wanting, whatever Mair said, to deflect her mother's attention from certain hard truths. She asked if they had a copy anywhere of Clifford's book; Angie stood blinking and absent from herself, as if she had no idea what Heloise meant. —Whose book?

—Dad's book. The whatsit of contemporary capitalism.

—Oh, *that* book. Good God. I've no idea. Why? You can't seriously be entertaining the idea of reading it?

—I just thought suddenly that I never have.

Toby said there was a whole box of them, under the bed in his old room. —They're a bit mummified, sort of shrunken and yellow.

—You can have all of them if you want, darling, Angie said. —Get rid of them for me.

—I don't want all of them, I only want one copy.

When Angie had gone to bed, Toby asked why Heloise wanted the book anyway, and she said that she'd been thinking about their father. He rumpled her hair affectionately; in childhood games she'd been her brother's faithful squire, in awe of his glamour as he advanced ahead of her into life, knowing all the things she didn't know. —I thought I went with Mum to France, she said, —after Dad's accident. But she told me no.

—Why would you have gone? Toby said. —None of us went. We had to stay with that ghastly family, the Philipses, and they were sanctimonious and sorry for us. I got drunk for the first time on their bottle of gin, really sick drunk, threw up all over their stair carpet, and they couldn't even be mad with me, under the circumstances. I can remember thinking at the time—this is awful really, considering Dad was dying—that from now on, under the circumstances, I could get away with just about anything.

Heloise said she'd been convinced, though, that she'd seen their dad in the hospital. —He looked so peacefully asleep, without his glasses: you know, how he was never peaceful in his life.

It was awful to think, she added, that their mother had travelled all alone to France.

—She wasn't alone. She had her boyfriend with her.

—What boyfriend?

—Terry? Jerry? That guy who kept his furniture here to sell it. I couldn't stand him.

—I'd forgotten about him. But that was just a business relationship—he wasn't her boyfriend.

—Oh yes he was.

Toby said that he'd once come across Angie "doing it," as he put it, in his mocking slangy drawl, with the stripped-pine dealer; this was in Clifford and Angie's bed, before the accident. Heloise was shocked and didn't want to believe it; but probably that sex scene was the kind of thing you couldn't make up, unlike a picture of your dead father at peace. And she did remember vaguely that Toby had fought with the furniture dealer, at some point in that awful time after Clifford's death—a real physical fight, here in this very kitchen. Toby said that effectively he'd won the fight, although Terry had knocked him down. Because it didn't look good, did it? Big beefy macho bloke beating up a skinny weak kid, his girlfriend's kid, making his nose bleed. Angie hadn't liked it. They hadn't seen much of Terry after that.

HELOISE BEGAN READING *RITES OF PASSAGE IN CONTEMPORARY Capitalist Societies* as soon as she got home that night. She seemed to hear her father's own voice—which she hadn't even realised she'd forgotten—right in her ear, urgent and confid-

ing. This sense of Clifford's closeness made her happy, just as
it used to when she was small and he read to her at bedtime,
or told her stories about his family or from history—she only
understood years later that he hadn't really ever been to Lvov or
Berlin or Moscow. He hadn't censored these stories or tamed
them to make them suitable for a child; he'd called her his
little scholar. His good moods couldn't be trusted, though; he
would come storming out of his study, ranting at the children,
if they made any noise when he was trying to write. Didn't
they care about his work, or believe it was important? Now
Heloise was reading the actual words he'd written, describing
the barrenness of life under consumer capitalism, the loss of
the meaning that was once created through shared belief and
ritual. And she seemed to see through, with miraculous ease,
to the flow of her father's thought.

When she picked up the book again, however, over her
coffee the next morning, while she waited for Richard to
bring back the children, she got bogged down in its technical
language: *the significance of changing notions of value for the development of a capitalist economy,* or, *the process of differentiation makes
sense if we see it as a continuous process of negotiation.* It would
take a huge mental effort on her part to even begin to master
Clifford's ideas, and she wasn't convinced, in her daylight self,
that it was worth it. She was afraid that, as the years had passed,
the relevance of his formulations might have slipped away, as
relevance had slipped from Toby's quiz. The book's pages had
an unread, depressing smell. In the end she lent it to Antony:
he was better with that kind of writing than she was. If he
felt like dipping into it, she said, she'd be interested to hear

whether he thought it was any good. She liked to think of Antony having her book in his safekeeping.

Then one stormy Thursday morning in half-term, Heloise turned up unannounced at Antony's house with Solly and Jemima. She had rung to ask him if they could come round, but his phone was switched off; in desperation, she'd decided to take a chance, drive over anyway. It had rained every day of the holiday so far, Richard was away, and Heloise had given up inventing things to do; often the children were still in pyjamas at teatime. Rain came sluicing across the big windows of their flat, the conifers thrashed at the end of the garden, wheelie bins blew over. Their rooms were like caves inside the rain, either greenish and spectral or bleak with the lights on in the middle of the day; the children crouched over their screens, whose colours flickered on their faces. Jemima accompanied back-to-back episodes of *Pet Rescue* on her violin; Solly played his Nintendo until he was glazed and drugged, shrugging Heloise off impatiently if she tried to touch him. The idea of Antony's ordered home was a haven in her imagination. He would be struggling to keep up with his work at home with his children, just as she was; only he was better at it, better at everything. His boys at this very moment, she thought, would be making art, or laughing at an old film. When Antony saw her, he'd know that she'd been trying her best, that the dreary shirt dress she'd put on was meant to be domesticated and sensible. She thought that it was time to make some offer of herself, to find a way to express how she wanted him.

His front door was down some stone steps, in a narrow basement area crowded with bikes, and tubs planted with herbs and shrubs; the muscular grey trunk of a wisteria wound up from here, branching across the whole front of the house. Heloise was worried—once they'd rung the bell and were waiting in the rain, which splashed loudly in the enclosed stone space—by not hearing the children inside. She didn't know what to do if Antony wasn't in. She was counting on him. Then the door opened and Delia stood there, in a grey wool dressing gown and nice red Moroccan leather slippers. She had those weathered, easy looks that are just as good in the morning, without make-up; she seemed taken aback when she saw Heloise, and, for one confused, outraged moment, Heloise thought that Delia's dismay was because she'd been caught out—Antony and Delia had been caught out together—in something forbidden and unforgivable. She knew perfectly well, in the next moment, that there was nothing forbidden about it. Antony could do what he liked. He didn't belong to her.

—Is Antony home?

—He just popped out, to buy bread for our breakfast. I thought you were him, coming back.

—Breakfast! Gosh, we've been up for hours.

Heloise knew how absurd she sounded, accusing them.

—Where are the boys?

The boys were with Antony's mother, not due back till after lunch. Heloise had blundered into what should have been a lazy lovers' breakfast: fresh rolls, butter, honey, scrolling through the news with sticky fingers, sharing stories. Imagining it, she was stricken with longing. Her children had been counting on their visit too: Jemima, whining, pressed her snotty face into

Heloise's thigh, Solly kicked at the wall and swore. —I *knew* there was no point in driving over.

—You'd better come in, Delia said. —I'll make coffee.

—You don't want visitors. We're the last thing you want.

—But you'd better come in. We ought to talk.

Heloise still thought that Delia meant they should talk about whatever was happening between her and Antony. The children were squeezing past her already, shedding wet coats, dropping to the floor in the hall to tug off their wellingtons, making a show of their eager compliance with house rules. Solly would be relishing the prospect of playing Max's games without Max; Jemima was in a phase of exploring other people's houses—she could spend hours staring into their cupboards and drawers, touching everything inside carefully, one item at a time. When Heloise followed Delia into the kitchen, she saw Clifford's book on the table. Delia stood facing her, with her hand on the book, in a gesture that was almost ceremonial.

—If this is your father, Delia said, —it makes a strange connection between us.

AT SOME POINT LATER, HELOISE TOLD HER MOTHER THE WHOLE story, though not about Delia moving in with Antony, not yet, in case her mother guessed that she'd had hopes herself. —There was no tree, she said. —Apparently they spun across two lanes and smashed into a lorry coming the other way. Delia doesn't remember this, but it's what they told her. You made up the tree. And it was Delia, after all, who was the lover; it wasn't the other one. The other one died.

Angie sat listening stiffly, cautiously, as if there were something bruising and dangerous in this news for her, even after all this time. —So what's she like then, the lover-girl?

Heloise said that she was hardly a girl. She wanted to say that Delia was cold and shallow and selfish, but she couldn't. —She's pretty tough. She's made a life for herself. I like her— she's a survivor.

—What does she look like? Is she scarred? I hope so.

She wasn't scarred, Heloise said, as far as she could see.

DELIA HAS NEVER BEEN ABLE TO REMEMBER ANYTHING FROM the time she and Clifford and Barbie set out for France until she woke up in hospital. Or just about woke up—into a long dream of pain, in which she was the prisoner of enemies speaking some alien language that was neither English nor French. Slowly, slowly, she'd come back from the dead. And now, after all these years, she can scarcely remember Clifford either, or why he had once seemed essential to her happiness. A few things: that he was over-exuberant making love, as if he were anxious to impress. That he was moved to tears when she played Brahms, though he claimed it was all over for nineteenth-century music. And the soft cleft shape of his chin, revealed when he'd shaved off his beard, disconcerting as if a third person, younger and more tentative, were in the bed alongside them. They had met at a concert: he was a friend of the father of someone she knew from the Guildhall.

But she can remember getting ready, in the flat she shared with Barbie, that morning they left for France. Clifford was expected any moment and Barbie was still packing, holding up one after another of the big-shouldered satiny dresses she wore, splashed with bright flower patterns, deciding which looked right for Paris, where she'd never been. Delia was anxious at the prospect of being without her violin for three whole days. She hardly thought about Clifford's wife and children, she discounted them; she was unformed and ignorant and very young, used to discounting whatever got in the way of her music. Was Delia sure, Barbie worried, that it was all right for her to travel with them? Didn't Delia and Clifford want to be alone together? Barbie promised she'd make herself scarce as soon as they got to Paris.

Delia wanted Barbie to come. Perhaps she was beginning to be tired of Clifford. Or perhaps she wanted to show off her grown-up lover to Barbie, who hadn't met him, or to show off Barbie to Clifford, have him see what lively, attractive friends she had. Barbie wasn't a musician, she was a primary-school teacher. She was a voluptuous blonde, effervescent and untidy, with thick calves and ankles, always in trouble because of her no-good boyfriends, or because she drank too much, or fell out over school policy with her head teacher. Climbing up onto the bed now, she was holding one of her dresses in front of her, singing and pretending to dance the can-can. In Delia's memory the window is open that morning in her bedroom, it's early spring, she's happy. The slanting low sunlight is dazzling in her dressing-table mirror.

Mia

ও

ALISON WAS DOING WELL IN HER A LEVEL SUBJECTS AT SCHOOL, but it didn't make her happy. She wanted to be beautiful. It was 1974 and she had a more or less clear ideal of beauty: hollow-eyed and scowling, dark and disabused and thin. She henna-ed her mouse-brown hair and grew it long; she wore print dresses from junk shops with men's suit waistcoats, and was saving her money for lace-up suede boots. She set herself strict targets for weight loss and daily intake of calories, then cheated. She and her mother were both small and square and seemingly irreducibly stocky, with frank round faces and pale freckled skin—because of their Irish peasant ancestry, her mother cheerfully explained. Her mother was a lecturer in sociology, and assured Alison that intelligence was what counted. But Alison used her intelligence to understand the poems and novels she read in English Literature, which told a different story.

At the same time as Alison was trying and failing to starve herself, she was acquiring a complete set of lavishly illustrated glossy Cordon Bleu cookbooks—*Hot Puddings, Meat Dishes,*

Cakes and Breadmaking and so on. And she was getting the money to pay for the cookbooks and the suede boots and other items by hiring herself out to cook for dinner parties at weekends. For a fee of ten pounds, on top of the cost of the food and a taxi home, she would design a menu, shop for the ingredients, cook the meal and serve it, as well as wash the dishes afterwards. She was much in demand among her mother's friends. It was a labour of twisted love. The meals as Alison planned them were flawless and joyous in her imagination. In reality, the work was difficult: the shopping bags were heavy, the washing-up took long ages, none of the food turned out as perfectly as in the books' glistening, seductive photographs, and she always ate too much of it.

Word got around about the dinner parties, and Alison began to be asked to do them for friends of her mother's friends, women she'd never actually met before. Someone called Mia asked her to come round to arrange something. Mia was a revelation. Even in the middle of an ordinary day in her own kitchen she wore a white dress slit to the thigh, with high heels and huge chequerboard earrings; she was very tall and very, very thin. Her coarse black hair was chopped off at shoulder length, her raw cheekbones seemed carved from rugged wood. She smoked French cigarettes and talked non-stop inconsequentially in a husky drawl. —I can't cook for toffee, she said. —I think you're awfully brave. I suppose you're brilliant in your lessons too. Alison tried to respond truthfully, but Mia wasn't interested in answers. She had grown up in Cairo during the war apparently; her mother was Greek and her father an Englishman. —That's why I'm so useless, she explained as if it were charming. —Because we always had servants to do everything.

Mia made Alison feel abjectly dowdy. However many pounds and stones she lost, whatever clothes she bought, she knew she'd never become whatever it was that Mia was: glamorous, fatal, unattainable. Because in the end it came down to temperament—Alison just didn't have it in her to be unattainable, she was too eager, and too sensible. Mia's home was a revelation too. Alison's family lived in a shabby terraced house with stripped-pine furniture and political posters drawing-pinned to the walls. Mia's husband—a small toady man with lips the colour of raw liver—was an architect, and their house was open-plan and split-level, with floor-to-ceiling glass doors that opened onto a patio overgrown with vines. The black glass dining table, in a sunken area where real water trickled through real ferns and pebbles, was at least out of sight—thank goodness—from the kitchen: which with its polished-steel cupboard-fronts and white surfaces looked more like the command deck of a spaceship than anywhere designed for real cooking. Alison decided to prepare most of the food in her own home; her mother would help her ferry it in the car to Mia's, where she'd give it the finishing touches. Smoked salmon and asparagus tartlets to begin with, Alison suggested. Chocolate and orange mousse with home-made almond tuiles for dessert. As for the main course . . .

Mia waved her hand heavy with rings, indifferent to the detail.

. . .

THE FEMALE GUESTS WERE AS SHRILL AND BRILLIANTLY PLUM-
aged as if the duller, plumper, preening males had herded a
flock of exotic birds into the ferny dining dell. Their high-
pitched pleasure floated back to the kitchen: Alison's puff pastry
was superbly crisp and buttery. Mia was serving up everything
herself, and taking all the credit for the cooking; it wasn't the
first time that had happened, and Alison didn't care. She got
a good look at the guests anyway, when she took in a forgotten dish of creamed potatoes. —This is Alison, gushed Mia.
—Terrifically brainy, she's been helping me out. Alison felt
on her skin a moment's dazzle of devouring looks, hungry for
sensation, before their bird-curiosity lapsed again. The toady
architect, carrying plates and trays somewhat unsteadily back
and forth, complimented Alison wholeheartedly on the food,
so that she forgave his clammy arm dropped on her shoulders,
his apologetic squeeze.

Taking advantage of the guests' long haul through the pork
served up in its rich sauce—it was braised with prunes in
Vouvray—she began filling the dishwasher; when she straightened up from slotting in plates she was startled to find a child
in the kitchen with her. An ugly pale boy aged seven or eight,
in pyjamas, stared at her out of protuberant colourless eyes
that were unmistakeably like his father's. She hadn't realised
there were any children. Usually you got warning from their
toys and photographs everywhere, their artwork proudly dis-
played: sugar paper stuck with pieces of pasta. Or their mother
would casually expect you to feed them, alongside managing

her dinner party. —Aren't you supposed to be in bed? Alison suggested unencouragingly.

Hanging on to the side of the breakfast bar, he slid soundlessly beneath it, until only his twin small knuckles were visible, strained white; when he'd been suspended there out of sight for a while he reversed the move strikingly, was at once upright again and still staring. —Not necessarily. No one said.

—What would your mother think? Alison tried.

He took that in and meditated upon it. Perhaps she had hit the right note—it wouldn't surprise her to learn that Mia was quite a disciplinarian. —She wouldn't mind, he decided eventually.

—Well, as long as you don't get under my feet. If you sit down you can have some chocolate pudding.

The boy explained regretfully that he only ever ate five things. He ticked them off on his fingers: digestive biscuits, Heinz lentil soup, pear, red Leicester cheese, and long-life orange juice without bits. And he could only eat and drink out of plain white china.

—You're a bit of a nuisance then, aren't you?

He said blandly that he supposed he was. —And what are you doing here?

—I'm working for your mother, helping out with her party.

Again he meditated. —Oh, I see, I get it. My mother: she's not much of a cook, is she?

—I wouldn't know, because I'm cooking tonight.

—Fair enough. Is this what you do for a living? Is it well

paid? Do you know what I want to be when I grow up? A forensic pathologist. Do you know what that is?

For a good half an hour the boy interrogated Alison relentlessly. Could she speak French as well as a French person? Did she believe in God? Had she ever heard of Bruce Lee? Did she think she could beat Bruce Lee in a fight?

—D'you like my mother? Do you think she's kind?

—I think she's very beautiful, Alison said truthfully.

Every time Mia or her husband came carrying dishes into the kitchen or fetching more food, or coffee, the boy performed his disappearing act, sliding out of sight under the breakfast bar, hanging there like a bat in a cave until they'd gone. Eventually, sternly, Alison ordered him up to bed. Somebody had to.

WHEN THE DINNER PARTY WAS ALL WOUND UP AND THE guests had departed and the architect—the worse for wear, drink-wise—had drifted upstairs, Mia came to talk to Alison in the kitchen. She perched on a high stool at the breakfast bar and her dress, made of some shiny purple stuff, hung from her hunched angular shoulders like bedraggled feathers; her eyelids, drooping in cavernous sockets, were painted a blaring magnificent green. All the dishes were washed and put away or burbling in the dishwasher, and Alison would have liked to call her taxi. —I'm so unhappy, Mia complained, waggling a cigarette between lips thick with plum colour, clicking at her lighter listlessly.

—But you have an amazing life.

She blew smoke through her nose. —Carl's lost all interest in me.

—You're so beautiful, you have this lovely home.

Mia checked her beauty reflexively in the stainless steel of a cupboard door. —But he won't talk to me, Alison. Also he doesn't want to have sex with me.

Alison was out of her depth with sex, her face was hot. And she didn't know how to raise the subject of her ten pounds plus taxi money. —At least you've got your little boy.

Mia stared blankly for a moment. —Oh—you mean the kid! You met the kid. Silly! The kid's not mine!

—I see . . .

Of course! That quirky froggy boy! How could Alison have imagined . . .

—Carl's first wife died, Mia explained. —Everything here is hers. I mean technically it isn't, obviously, because she's dead. But it's really a Rebecca situation—did you ever see that film? Quite boring actually. *The first Mrs. de Winter* . . . And Carl's first wife was such a brainbox! All her books! Bronze Age whatnot, bullfights, gardening. I hate books. I ought to give them to you, Alison. I'm such an ignoramus. In Cairo . . .

But something stopped her in mid-flow, perplexed as if an idea eluded her that might be important. —What did Jerome say to you anyway? That's the kid's name. Did he say anything about me? Was he complaining? Because I've tried, I've really tried, to be a mother to him. But you know, he doesn't . . . She made a visible, shuddering effort of comprehension, jangling her earrings. —He doesn't open up.

Alison thought carefully before she spoke, shrugging her coat across her shoulders. —I think he's fond of you.

—Do you think so? Mia's huge eyes overflowed unexpectedly with emotion, so that she had to staunch them with a tissue. —Do you really think so? He's a weird little kid. But I suppose that I've got used to having him around.

—You should take him out somewhere, Alison suggested. —To the zoo or something.

Mia brightened up, prodding out her cigarette in one of the leftover smoked-salmon tartlets. —You see, you are clever! That's a good idea. Because I always used to love the zoo.

She insisted on driving Alison home in her Aston Martin, swearing she was sober as a judge. There was a swollen dirty moon and the parks were milky with mist. —Why don't you cut your hair off short? Mia suggested, as if she'd been giving it some serious thought. —Boyish, a sort of pixie cut. It would suit you better. And when they pulled up outside Alison's house she leaned across to the passenger seat to demonstrate, cupping her hands over Alison's ears, making a sawing motion against her neck. Alison didn't like Mia really, but she melted at that touch—grown-up woman to woman. —I hope you have fun at the zoo, she said. Mia agreed vaguely, as if she'd already half-forgotten about that plan.

Coda

I WENT UPSTAIRS IN MY MOTHER'S HOUSE, TELLING HER I WAS going to the bathroom. There was a downstairs toilet, but it had a raised seat and a frame with armrests so that she could easily manoeuvre herself on and off after her hip replacement, and I was squeamish about it. I couldn't help feeling irrationally that if I used it I'd be contaminated with something: with suffering, with old age. And anyway I didn't really need to use the bathroom. I went into the one upstairs that was free of any apparatus, closed the door and sat on the toilet-seat lid, then pressed the flush so that she could hear it. The truth was that every so often I just needed to be alone for a few minutes, not making any effort, or being filled up with anyone else's idea of what I was.

Don't get me wrong. First of all, my mother wasn't really suffering, she was getting along pretty well for ninety-two. She had magical powers, I sometimes thought, of resilience and brightness. And I was glad to be with her during that time when we were all locked down, month after month, because of the coronavirus. I couldn't have been happy living away from her, worrying about how she was managing by herself, knowing she must be lonely. She had friends who would shop for her, plus a cleaner and someone to keep the garden tidy— and these people were her friends too, although she paid them. But she was naturally sociable, and longed for company— any company, even mine. We had both lost our men, hers to death three years earlier: her third husband, Dickie, not my father, who was her first and had died long before. And mine to divorce, at about the same time. We grieved for them, but it was also restful without them, without the performance and the competition that they brought. My mother was old-fashioned in that way, a man's woman. She used to flirt even with my husband. I'll have to call her Margot. I can't just go on calling her *my mother*, as if that were all she was.

Treading quietly in my stocking feet, I went into the spare bedroom at the front of the house, overlooking the street. This wasn't where I slept—I preferred the couch in the dark little den behind it, which had shelves with a few books on them and was supposed to have been Dickie's study, though I don't know what studying he ever did. Studied the bottom of a wine glass perhaps. He'd set up their BT hub and computer in there, although the height of his achievement on the Internet, as far as I could see, was forwarding comical YouTube videos. My mother disdained the new technology and still wrote her letters in elegant longhand, at a small desk downstairs she called her *bureau*. My mother, Margot. You'd have thought she'd been brought up in the leisured classes, drinking tea out of fine china, you'd never have guessed that her parents were a factory worker and a cleaner. Not that she was in denial of her past, or not exactly; she didn't pretend to be anything she wasn't. When she told the old stories of her childhood in Liverpool, her eyes filled up with genuine tears of remembrance and nostalgia: she was quite lovely then. She had made a whole life out of being lovely, even if she always disparaged her looks. *I know what classic beauty is, darling. All I have is personality.* In the fifties, before she married, she had worked modelling clothes—and was even in a couple of films, although she couldn't act. It was a shame that in my looks I took after my father, who was a producer on one of those films.

This spare bedroom was a secret space, a nothingness: freedom. The radiator was turned off in there and the door was kept shut, its chill was a relief from the dry heat in the rest of the house. I don't think anyone had ever slept in its double bed. Cardboard boxes, piled up on the carpet and on the bare mattress, were filled with pairs of shoes and empty coat-hangers, jazz vinyl from the sixties and seventies, unwanted gifts of hand lotion and scented candles still wrapped in dusty cellophane. Files bulged with papers from the little business Dickie had importing wine, which never made any money, perhaps because he drank so much of it; there were more boxes of these papers in the garage, and his children had been promising to sort them out, until lockdown gave them an excuse for not coming to do it. Fitted wardrobes were full with the overspill of Margot's clothes, coats and dresses swathed in plastic as they'd come from the dry-cleaners.

She'd moved to this unfashionable seaside town ten years ago, when she was already in her eighties and Dickie was older.

Of all the places for her to end up, this might have seemed the most improbable, considering where she'd lived in her long lifetime: Cap-Ferrat, Manhattan, the Bahamas, Rome. For a while with her second husband—*the boring banker*, she called him now—she moved between a house in Chelsea and an oversized villa in the woods in Deeside, sunk in a tidal wave of rhododendrons. But she'd run out of money years ago: the boring banker turned out to be vengeful when it came to divorce, and whatever was left Dickie had invested in his business. So they'd found themselves here in Cherry Tree Lodge, in these rooms crowded with too much furniture that belonged somewhere bigger and showier, tucked·in among neighbours offering Bed and Breakfast, in a dull terraced street of modestly sized conforming houses, faced in frigid grey stone, without even a view of what wasn't actually the sea in any case, but only the silt-brown Bristol Channel between England and Wales.

Margot didn't mind it really. I think it was Dickie who hated it and felt it was a comedown. But who wanted to be an old woman in a fashionable place? It was better to exert her fascination here, where nobody else was like her. And anyway she knew what I knew, from growing up in Cap-Ferrat and the Bahamas and the rest: every place, even if it's not at all glamorous, has its own secrets and seductions. The most glamorous places may be the least secretive, the most blank. And, incidentally, I'm exaggerating the privations in Margot's past. Her parents weren't really very poor, or at least not for long. Her father had a good job in a factory where they made precision tools for aeronautics, and her mother was only a cleaner for a while, when she was first married and before she had Margot—who was christened Margaret but didn't like it. When I knew my grandmother, in her middle age, she was a stout, short, tidy, wary person, the manager of a Liverpool branch of the Wool Shop, which was the place where I was most purely happy as a child. The fresh new balls of wool gave me a frisson that was decidedly sensual: all arranged in their ordered gradations of colour and type, with that pristine stuffy smell, and the pattern books holding out their promise. Later, when I was pregnant with my son, I knitted tiny vests and cardigans on fine needles, in two-ply cream pure wool, fastening in front with baby ribbon ties or teeny mother-of-pearl buttons. These things turned out to be useless once I had the actual baby. They had to be washed by hand every time he sicked up on them; then he developed eczema and couldn't wear wool anyway.

THE FRONT WINDOW IN THAT SPARE ROOM LOOKED OUT INTO the branches of the cherry tree that grew in the narrow gravelled strip of its front garden and gave its name to the house. In the spring, when lockdown was new and the weather, in consolation or mockery, was so uncannily beautiful week after week, this tree had blazed with its great burden of blossom, the white flowers' crimson hearts leaking pink stain into the frail material of the petals, an incongruous poem in a prosaic street. But now the branches of the tree were bare, the weather was wintry, we were back in lockdown; when I stood at the window I felt a warning chill coming off the glass. It was three o'clock on a November's afternoon and I hadn't turned on the light. Already the air outside seemed blue with evening; the wilted shrubs in the front gardens and the double row of parked cars were desolate, shrouded in cold. I thought at first that there was no one out there. I treasured these passages of astringent solitude, stolen from my day.

Then I saw that I wasn't alone after all. A woman was standing beside the wheelie bins in the paved front area next door, smoking a cigarette. I hadn't noticed her at first because she stood almost directly below me—I was looking down now at the top of her head, into the thick mass of her black hair. Her back was more or less turned to me, she couldn't possibly have seen me, and I'm sure I'd have been invisible to her anyway, even if she'd chosen to look up behind her; the windowpanes would only have reflected darkness. Nonetheless, I took a step away from the window, which was steaming up from my breath on the cold glass. This woman's character seemed strongly expressed in her physical presence. With her shoulders tensed and her head held back defiantly, as if she expected to be challenged, she flaunted her cigarette, wrist angled coquettishly, turning her face away to blow out smoke. Her black coat with its fake-fur collar was shrugged on against the cold; beneath it, she had on a white housecoat like a nurse's uniform, which made me think she must be some sort of carer for the old man next door. We didn't know him very well, we'd spoken to his grown-up sons going in and out, I'd offered to do shopping for him but they said they could manage. I guessed that this carer was pent-up like me, bracing herself for a return to the daily perpetual work of kindness. She sucked on that cigarette thirstily, holding her right elbow in her left hand, left arm clasped tightly against her body. When she'd finished she ground out the cigarette end under her heel.

Before she went inside she cast one quick look up at our window, which made me start back again; I was sure she couldn't have seen me, but she might have an animal intuition that she was being watched. And as she punched the buttons on the key safe before unlocking the door and disappearing into the house, I had time to see that she was much younger than me, but not young. Forty perhaps, with something faded or hardened in her smudged, brash, sultry looks—snub nose, full mouth, luxuriant thick lashes, scarred bad skin. With her stocky build and dark colouring, she might have been Spanish or Portuguese. Margot wouldn't have considered this woman in the least pretty or sexy; she'd have said that she was coarse. *I can see how some people might find her attractive.* Her judgement on such matters was always inflexible, with that little twist of distaste in her face, behind the show of concession and self-doubt.

—What were you doing in the spare room? she asked when I went downstairs.

—I went to the loo, I said. —I went to look out of the window.

—Anything happening out on Desolation Row?

—Nothing, no. No one.

I WAS READING *MADAME BOVARY* IN TRANSLATION. OFTEN AT night I couldn't sleep: we spent quite a lot of time in bed at Cherry Tree Lodge and I wasn't used to it—after lunch every day we went to our rooms for a nap, Margot riding upstairs with aplomb on her Stannah stairlift. I'd found this stumpy little paperback among the travel books and humour and wine guides on the shelves in Dickie's study, its paper rough and yellowed, its cover all ripped bodice and turbulent passion, no hint of the novel's irony. It must have been Margot's, though I don't know why she had that ugly copy. She loved novels and claimed to have read the whole of Proust one summer in the South of France, though these days she preferred thrillers; perhaps Dickie had been deceived by the cover and borrowed it, hoping for salaciousness inside. There was salaciousness inside, of course, but not his kind. The glue on the novel's spine had cracked, and its pages fell out as I read, propped up against pillows in the narrow put-me-up, tilting the book so that it caught the weak light from Dickie's desk lamp, brown crumbs of brittle glue sprinkling on the sheet. But they'd used the old Steegmuller translation and nothing could spoil the ferocious pure aim of the words, right at the heart of reality.

I knew what must become of these characters, and yet I felt their jeopardy on the page just as if they were free, making up their lives as they went along, hesitating over choosing this path rather than that one, Emma Bovary making such a fool of herself although she thought she was so special, with her restlessness and devouring, hectic need. I only turned the light out that first night when I heard Margot get up to use her little en suite, I didn't want her worrying about my wakefulness. And then the next night and the next, as soon as I went to bed, I picked up *Madame Bovary* again—although for some reason I didn't want to bring it downstairs, or have Margot know that I was reading it. She would have been pleased, she'd have gone into ecstasies over how much the book meant to her and how marvellous the writing was. She said the things I read were much too dry. But since I was a child I'd had an instinct—which probably made me furtive, and difficult to love—to keep my inner life out of my mother's sight. For the moment *Madame Bovary* was my inner life, stirred like rich jam into the blandness of my days.

Meanwhile, I'd be coaxing Margot to eat her breakfast. She always declared she was starving and gave precise instructions as to what she wanted—Earl Grey tea and orange juice with triangles of buttered rye toast and honey—then ran out of appetite halfway through the first piece of toast. I sorted out her pills and watched to make sure she swallowed them, because she was full of private superstitions about her health; her doctors in their reports called her *this delightful elderly lady,* but she was sceptical of their strict instructions and carelessly forgot them. When I helped put in her hearing aids, she flinched and pulled her head away. —Ouch, Diane! Be careful, darling. Dickie was so gentle when he did them.

Her white hair was very fine and straight, and she wore it swept into a chignon which I was allowed to pin, while she grimaced into the mirror as if I were skewering her. Then she *put on her face* as she called it, sitting at her dressing table, attending with religious seriousness to making up *that awful old woman* in the reflection. Not that she was awful. Some beauties, it's true, are simply extinguished as age descends, but the same old light was still shining in Margot, despite the drooping earlobes she loathed, the age-spots, the tremulous pouting lower lip. These were part of her now, and the light shone through them. She'd kept the nervous fine line of her jaw, and the striking straight nose, and what the magazines call poise. People often thought she'd been a dancer.

By the time we were both dressed, and she'd done her make-up and I'd washed the breakfast dishes, we were ready for morning coffee. You mustn't imagine that we were mute or dull, as we worked through these daily tasks. We were both talkers, although our conversational styles were very different. Margot's flow of chatter was punctuated by my glum debunking remarks, my jokes, my good grasp of facts. Truly I was glad to have someone to talk to, just as she was. It was Margot who kept our spirits up. Although she was bound to be sad sometimes without Dickie, the compass in her nature was set to cheerfulness. And she wasn't one of those elderly ladies who go on about the old days either. She took a sharp interest in current affairs and insisted on watching the news, although she did get muddled about the facts; even when she was younger she hadn't been all that strong on facts. No one required you to understand progressive taxation or the American electoral college if you looked like Margot. —The trouble with the old days, Diane, she said, —is that when you put me into the home it'll be wall-to-wall Fred Astaire and Ginger Rogers, or ghastly singalongs to Vera Lynn. But those were my mother's old days, not mine. I prefer Nina Simone.

—All right, then, I won't put you into a home after all, I said, deadpan.

—Not unless you can find one that plays Nina Simone.

We were observing the lockdown fairly strictly, no one

came to the house, although we went on paying the cleaner because she had to manage somehow. We left the gardener's money outside in an envelope and waved at him through the window. From time to time Margot forgot about the rules, and suggested with bright enthusiasm that we go out somewhere for a treat, for afternoon tea or—even better!—a drink, a nice strong martini in a country pub. When I had to remind her that we weren't allowed out, and all the cafés and pubs were closed, she remembered at once, but you could still see the shock on her face—partly shock at herself, because she'd been found out as a silly old woman. Also shock because she couldn't have what she wanted, which was only what she'd wanted all her life: happiness and fun. But she was courageous, and tried to hide her disappointment from me.

I ought to come clean about something. You may be thinking I was pretty self-sacrificing, giving up my own life to come down to the seaside during lockdown, to look after my ageing mother and sort out her bills and her mail, cook her meals, sit with her every evening in front of the telly turned up very loud with the subtitles on. But the fact was that at that point my own life wasn't much to write home about. Since my divorce things hadn't gone well for me. I'd taken early retirement from the FE college where I'd taught, and then I couldn't afford the mortgage payments on the flat I'd moved into. I let things get into such a mess that in clarifying moments I used to think, *No wonder he divorced me.* My son and his wife wanted me to go and live with them while I sorted myself out, and they're possibly the people I love best in the world (along with my mother of course), but I dreaded having them get tired of me. And I'd been spending more time down at Margot's anyway, helping out now she was on her own. So it made perfect sense to move in with her when the lockdown began. From a selfish point of view, the pandemic couldn't have arrived at a better moment.

I WAS GETTING TO KNOW THE ROUTINES OF THE WOMAN I'D seen next door. She seemed to be there every weekday from about eight o'clock—the old man's sons turned up for an hour or two at weekends. Sometimes she came on foot in her high heels, which she changed for slip-ons at the front door; sometimes she arrived in a low-slung blue car, with one door panel sprayed a different colour, a souped-up noisy engine, and chrome hubcaps. She would put her head in the car window to say goodbye and linger there talking, reluctant to part with whoever was inside; the smile on her face, when she straightened up, was sleek and replete in a way that made me think he must be a lover or new boyfriend. Then she put on her mask and sanitised her hands before going into the house. In my mind she got mixed up sometimes with Emma Bovary, although they surely weren't in any way alike. Emma was young, and was exceptional and graceful enough to attract Rodolphe, privileged connoisseur of women. This middle-aged carer next door was short, with a full figure and thick ankles.

Every couple of hours during the day she popped out for a smoke in the front garden, with her mask pulled down under her chin. She was sometimes on her phone as she smoked, talking intently into it, chiding and severe with some callers—

her ex? her teenage children?—then charming and flirting when she was talking, I could only assume, to her boyfriend. She performed for him as if she could be seen, twisting on her heel or stepping from foot to foot, throwing back her head to laugh, showing white strong teeth, bright eyes. There was something second-hand in this performance of sex allure, as if she'd copied it from TV or films, yet the artificiality was also part of her attraction. I was starting to make a point of going upstairs whenever I thought she might be outside. And I realised that she went out into the back garden in the afternoons, if the weather was dry, taking her patient for a walk. The thin, tall old man, with his pink-and-white baby freshness, would lean heavily on her shoulder, angular like a lopsided crane, grasping his stick in his other hand or fumbling with the disposable mask, which slipped off his beak-sharp nose. He'd been a keen gardener before his stroke; when Margot and Dickie first moved in, they'd made a joke out of skulking indoors, to avoid getting into conversation with him—he was always trying to give them cuttings. Margot felt guilty about it now. *I expect the poor man was just missing his wife.*

His carer bore up underneath him sturdily, taking his weight. I watched them from the window in Dickie's study, keeping out of sight behind the curtain. Her demeanour was quite different then, from how she was alone or on her phone. How patient she was, progressing at the old man's slow pace, collapsing her own will and subordinating it to his need; and she was cheerfully encouraging, taking care not to condescend to him. They went from plant to plant and he tried to tell her about them, she pretended to be interested. It was a mystery that some people had this gift of caring. I'd heard this woman on her phone and she wasn't in the least a saint: she could be harsh, or shallow. God knows what her politics were. Yet I had a hunch that in a crisis, right down at the bottom of life, where all the trivial judgements about taste and personality and class no longer count for anything, she had the right hands to ease and comfort you.

As a carer, she actually added something of value in the world, which is more than Emma Bovary ever did. She was kind to old Mr. Hansen, and competent, and worked hard for a living, no doubt underpaid by some agency raking in their profits. And yet I felt sure that she was possessed by that same divine restlessness, or whatever power it was that sent Madame Bovary off in the early morning, making her way shamelessly to visit her lover, dragging her full skirts through the soaked fields. Our neighbour's carer exuded this surplus energy; even watching her attending patiently to the old man, I seemed to feel it coiling off her like heat. She had her life as a carer, and she had this other secret life, concealed inside it. Or perhaps the surplus energy was all mine. At first my breathlessness when I thought of her was only a game, like the crushes I used to have at school. I hurried upstairs in the hope of seeing her, contriving reasons for it cunningly, because Margot must not be allowed any clue as to what was going on. My fixation helped to pass the time, the long empty days.

I hadn't felt anything like this for years. And in those school-girl crushes, too, I hadn't really wanted consummation—or recognition, even, from the beloved one. I had just wanted to feel faint with worship, whisking past the object of my desire

in the school corridors between lessons, while she was hurrying in the opposite direction, and was agitatedly, keenly—
glancing around for teachers, because we weren't supposed to
talk in the corridors—pouring gossip into some friend's ear.
Not gossip about me. She didn't even know that I existed.
Or I'd watch her swivelling on one foot on the netball court,
holding the ball tensely on her shoulder before throwing it, so
that the little skirt of her gym tunic flared with her movement.
I was never the one who caught the ball. I was never in the
right place at the right time.

ONCE A WEEK I WAS DRIVING TO THE SUPERMARKET TO STOCK
up on food. I could have ordered the shopping online but,
although I wasn't in the least resentful of Margot, I appreciated
an opportunity to get out of the house, play Radio 4 in the car
for ten minutes each way without any need to comment, and
have my thoughts to myself as I piled our usual items in the
shopping trolley. One late afternoon I met my Emma Bovary
in the Morrisons car park at dusk. It was the shortest day in
the year, and the wind was gusting frozen sleety rain in our
faces, slicking the plastic carriers. She was on her way out as
I was going in; we were both wearing our masks, but I'd have
recognised her anywhere. I heard the chink of bottles in her
bag, and felt almost tenderly as though they were kin to the
bottles I'd be picking out from the shelves myself, any minute
now. Margot and I were getting through the martinis at a rate,
in the evenings.

To my surprise I found myself stopping in front of her,

blocking her way. Affronted, head down against the rain, she tried to get past me.

—Hello, I said. —I think I know you.

No recognition when she raised her head to look at me, eyes as blank as the dark windows where I'd stood watching her. She was impatient, because I was preventing her from getting out of the rain into her car: that low-slung blue car, perhaps. And was she driving it this time, or was her man waiting in it? —You're looking after our neighbour, I said. —Mr. Hansen. I see you with him sometimes in the garden.

She seemed to arrange her face then into an expression of guarded minimal pleasantness, appropriate for dealing with someone of the employer class; of course I could only see her eyes. Her mask was one of those black ones made of stretch material, faintly suggestive and sinister, like a carnival mask. —Mr. Hansen's a lovely old gent, she said. —I'm very fond of him.

—You're very nice to him.

—He likes to get out there with his plants. So which of those houses is yours?

How constrained her voice was, compared with when I'd heard her wheedling and teasing on her phone. I was eager to abolish the distance and class divide between us. —It's not my house, I said, which was, after all, strictly true. —I'm in with the old lady at number seven, looking after her.

She looked at me oddly then, and more penetratingly. It must have been because I was wearing my own mask that I was able to utter these half-lies, as if they could be made innocuous, filtered through the cloth over my mouth. —I thought there was a daughter, she said. All this time she was backing away from me through the nasty weather, towards her car parked nearby; I was aware of a blur of blue somewhere at the edge of my vision. I waved my hand at her as if the daughter were a long story.

—Do you know them, then? I called. —Do you know Margot? She's had the first shot of her vaccination. How about Mr. Hansen?

—We're booked in for tomorrow, she said. The car boot sprang open, operated from inside the car; she lifted her bags to put them in, raising her voice above the rain. —I do know Margot, yes. Not very well.

THEN IT WAS CHRISTMAS, AND AFTER CHRISTMAS IT RAINED for a week, so there wasn't much opportunity for spying. Our neighbour's carer opened the front door when she wanted a cigarette and stood just inside it, so that I could only see her hand wafting the smoke away; when she arrived in the mornings I looked down into the tortured black nylon of her umbrella with its broken rib. I was sometimes aware of her and Mr. Hansen moving around inside the house, and if I put my ear to the wall I could hear their voices dimly, or their TV turned up loud like ours. As soon as the weather was better I watched out for them in the back garden. One morning after coffee we went up to Margot's bedroom at the back of the house; Margot was longing, she said, to have a go at my hair. Sitting in her place at the dressing table, I stared stoically at both our reflections; she stood behind me with an inspired

face, sifting her hands through my grey-brown hair like a professional—it had grown out of its cut, into long lumps like
spaniel ears. Outside a mass of cloud was refulgent with gold
light, and a bitter wind scoured the blue sky; twiggy winter
trees bent under it stiffly. Concentrating on the problem of my
lack of allure, Margot glanced inadvertently into the next-door
garden, then let go my hair in dismay.

—Christ, it's that woman! Don't look at her, Diane.

—What woman? I said, getting up to look, keeping out of
sight behind the curtains.

—I don't know, whatshername, Teresa.

Mr. Hansen was being taken for his walk in all the wind
and flashing sunshine, wrapped up in his overcoat and scarf,
leaning on his carer. She seemed to lift her face toward our
window when they turned at the end of the path. Margot was
cowering excitedly, bobbing behind my shoulder. —She used
to look after Dickie when he was poorly.

—Really? I don't remember her.

—Well, she was one of the ones who came. I didn't like her
one bit; I wish the Hansens had asked me before they hired
her. She tried to make Dickie go out in all weathers too, but
he hated it.

—It would have done him good. He was supposed to exer-
cise. He got too fat.

—It was torture for the poor man. He could have caught
his death of cold.

—He died of cirrhosis of the liver.

—No thanks to Teresa.

Sitting down again at the dressing table, I was reassured

when I saw in the mirror my composed imperturbable surface, its habitual heavy severity between the spaniel ears. —She looks Mediterranean, I said. —Is she Portuguese?

—Maltese. Her parents were Maltese, I believe.

I rolled her name voluptuously around inside my mind. Teresa. And Malta fitted too somehow: my idea of it, Catholic, militaristic, patriarchal. —And you dislike her just because she made Dickie go outside?

Margot tried to go back to my hair, but when she rested her hands on my head I felt them trembling. —She took money.

I was shocked and half-thrilled, and said she should be careful before she went around making that sort of accusation. —Are you sure, Mum? Do you mean you left money lying around and it was gone? But half the time you've no idea how much is in your purse.

—Dickie gave her money.

—How do you know?

—I found the stubs in the chequebook. He thought I never looked in there. It wasn't just her pay. There were separate sums, over and above. He only wrote T, but I'm sure those payments were for her; he pretended he couldn't remember, when I asked him. Not that much money: twenty-five pounds here, fifty there.

She looked meaningfully at my reflection in the mirror. Margot had adored Dickie, he was the one she'd loved best of all her husbands: faded and drawling and handsome, he'd had that deprecating Englishness which melted her (my father was Czech and a Jew, the boring banker a Scot). Like her, he'd got by all his life on his looks and his charm, and there was an almost feminine camaraderie to their intimacy: Dickie fastened the clasps of her necklaces and did up her zips and pinned her hair skilfully, advising her on her outfits. I remembered the ambulancemen carrying him out from the house for the last time, strapped into a stretcher-chair, insisting in his delirium that he had important calls to make.

—So what was he paying her for?

—What do you think?

I don't know why I felt a surge of cruelty towards her then. Usually Margot couldn't wait to talk about sex, lit up with the naughtiness and the scandal of it: she teased me for being puritanical. It was fervid in her generation, their conviction that sex was behind everything—she derived her force from it, and her validation. *Men can't help themselves, darling. I know what girls that age are like. You should flaunt that nice figure of yours, not hide it away.* I wanted to laugh at this story of Dickie and make light of it, although it was clearly painful to her.

—Do you mean that he was paying her for sex?

—I think she let him touch her. Nothing under the clothes: that's what he insisted when I confronted him. He held her, she let him put his head against her. He wasn't capable by that time, let's be honest, of much more. It was an infatuation—he was a sick man. He didn't know what he was doing.

She couldn't stop giving me all this, spitting it out viciously, now she'd begun—getting rid of a blockage of secret knowledge, which had been poisoning her. I couldn't work out at first why she hadn't told me before; it would have been just her sort of story if it had been about someone else, and she'd made me wince often enough in the past, with her frankness over her sex life. Perhaps she hadn't wanted me to think less of Dickie. But then I realised that if she was scalding with shame, it wasn't on Dickie's behalf. In her world, if there was shame anywhere in a sex transaction, it always stuck to the woman. When a man was unfaithful, the disgrace of it was somehow with the woman who'd failed to hang on to him. Hadn't she made a lovely home for him? Wasn't she keeping herself up? Wasn't she any good in bed? If Dickie had done anything with Teresa, it would have shamed my mother, gouging out wounds in her self-respect, even though he was a bent old man who couldn't dress himself. He could have touched her, but he'd preferred someone else.

—I went through the bank statements. I don't think she even cashed those cheques.

—Nobody uses cheques these days, Mum. They're more of a nuisance than they're worth. I'll bet they were nothing to do with her.

—Or she took them just to humiliate us. That's what I couldn't forgive.

I thought that Teresa might have been humouring an old man. She might have put her arms round him in the ordinary course of her caring duties, and she might have refused the extra cheques at first, and then when he made a fuss, taken them just to please him, with no intention of ever cashing them. Or the Teresa who cavorted on the phone for her lover, and ground out cigarettes under her heel, may have taken her own twisted pleasure in the uncashed cheques. Perhaps they gave her a leverage in her thoughts, against these employers who'd fallen into the slough of old age from such superior heights of elegance and wealth. Or perhaps the cheques were simply Dickie's mistakes, screwed up and thrown in the waste-paper basket. Anyhow we listened, and after a while heard her take Mr. Hansen inside, close the back door. We gave up on the project of my hair.

IN SOME CALMLY RELINQUISHING WAY, WHEN I CAME DOWN to live with my mother I had been thinking that my life was over. No, that's not it, it wasn't *over*. Most likely, as I had my health and my strength, it would carry on for a number of years. For a few years, or a lot—who knew which to hope for? We were taking every precaution against catching the virus. But at any rate the story of my life was set down, its themes were established, and I was living in the coda. With that acceptance came relief. There was something decent in it.

Yet sometimes I woke, those mornings at the seaside, to such anguished intimations of loss. It couldn't be over! How could my life be gone, before I'd even had it? I hadn't had drama or joy or passion: those things were real, and other people had them, but not me! This protest came from some deep place in my sleep, inside a dream, and as I surfaced into wakefulness it seemed at first overwhelming, an unassuageable thirst. Then my rationalising self began the cover-up, pacifica-tion. I was embarrassed by my greedy ego. You're safe, I told myself. You're so lucky, you're privileged. You've had your share of happiness, you've had your child. I anchored myself there, in the thought of my beloved child, my son—now a middle-aged man of forty, sane and good. The dream evaporated anyway, as I tried to fix it in consciousness. But I knew that somewhere hidden inside it, so intense and precise that they felt like memory, were the sensations of bliss, and love, and touching.

IN MY ROOM ONE AFTERNOON, WRAPPED IN A BLANKET ON MY bed, I got lost inside *Madame Bovary:* the novel was winding towards its awful ending. Margot and I must have gone upstairs for our nap at about two thirty; when I put the book down it was after four, and dark outside. I realised that I hadn't heard Margot getting up. Throwing back the rug and not stopping to put on my shoes, I hurried along to her room, calling her name as I opened the door, in a low voice in case she was still asleep. In the light from the landing I saw her lying motionless where she'd fallen, a pale shape face down on the carpet, with her foot in a tangle of sheets and blankets. Her position looked oddly hieratic, very straight with her arms at her sides, improbable and theatrical as if she'd adopted it for some tableau, or to make a point. In a tumult of dread and recognition, I was sure that she was dead.

And I ran next door. In my stocking feet I thudded downstairs and out into the street, drawing raw jolting breaths, barely aware that it was raining and my feet were soaked at once in dirty puddled water. I pressed Mr. Hansen's bell and banged on his door with my fist. —Help me, please help me. At such extreme moments all shyness and awkwardness drop away. I must have looked like a madwoman. —Please help me, I said, when Teresa opened the door. —My mother's fallen in the bedroom.

She was wearing her short white nurse's housecoat, wiping her hands on a tea towel; I'd interrupted her in the middle of her tasks. I longed for her composure and sturdy competence, and didn't care just then about any history between her and Dickie, or my own performance in the car park; she wasn't surprised to hear that I was Margot's daughter. She was ready at once for an emergency, letting Mr. Hansen know she was only going next door, so that he wasn't anxious. Everything seemed unreal as we hurried inside Cherry Tree Lodge together, and I led the way upstairs. When I was young my fantasies of love had often been staged in the context of some crisis or disaster like this, in which the usual fixed hierarchy and rules of conduct were suspended. I explained how Margot and I had gone up for our nap, then I'd woken to find her on the floor. The scene in the bedroom was as dramatic as when I'd left it, Margot hadn't moved. She'd lain down for her nap in her petticoat, and when I switched on the light her bare arms and legs looked blue-white like skimmed milk, curdled and dimpled with age. Her feet were purplish, their shape distorted with swelling, but that was nothing new. Her long hair, unpinned from its chignon, was fanned out over the floor; the flesh of her face was squeezed against the carpet. —Margot? I said, kneeling beside her. —Mum?

—I've been here all night, she said into the carpet, muffled, indignant.

—You haven't. It's only teatime, it's four o'clock. How did you fall? Have you hurt yourself? What hurts?

—It was awful, Diane, I was calling you. Why couldn't you hear me?

TERESA WAS SO TACTFUL AND CONSIDERATE WITH MY MOTHER, introducing herself and asking permission before she touched her. She felt for her pulse, and smoothed away the white hair where it fell over my mother's eyes. *Such lovely hair.* And she put her hand tenderly on the purple feet, which were ice-cold.

—I know who you are, Margot said. —You can't fool me.

—I'm working next door, for your neighbour Mr. Hansen. Diane asked for my help when she found that you'd fallen.

—I don't need anyone's help. I just want to be back in my own bed.

Teresa explained to me that she knew my mother because she'd worked in this house, looking after my dad when he was poorly; no doubt I sounded as ungracious as Margot when I insisted to Teresa that Dickie wasn't my dad. I saw how Teresa let the rudeness roll over her with trained indifference, looking past it to the patient's need. We weren't sure if we ought to try to lift her, but Margot said she wasn't bloody well staying down there, with her face in the carpet.

—Can you move your arms? Can you wiggle your feet?

Grudgingly Margot obliged: she hurt all over, but everything just about worked. We phoned the emergency services, a doctor rang back, we gave her details again and again and they said it was okay to try to get her up, and to give her painkillers. While we waited for the paramedics to arrive, between us we managed to help Margot first onto her side, and then up and into the bathroom because she needed to pee, then into bed, where we propped her on pillows and she was more comfortable. She seemed to have sprained her shoulder and bruised her ribs when she fell, and bruised both her knees, and that was all; it could have been so much worse. I found her some paracetamol. —I'm not going into hospital, she said.

—Probably you won't have to, Teresa said cheerfully. —I don't think you've broken anything. But better have the paramedics check you over, just to be on the safe side. You never know.

—But I hate the safe side! The safe side's so boring!

Whenever Margot was ill at ease she put on a show of hauteur, exaggerating the posh accent she must have acquired when she was a girl in London, making her way in modelling. I think she even had elocution lessons. She hissed at me furiously when Teresa's back was turned. —I didn't want her to see me like this.

—You've had an accident, I said. —Nobody cares how you look.

I hadn't bothered to change my own tights, which were still wet and dirty from the rain. Even in that overheated house I was shivering. When Teresa said she ought to go back to be with Mr. Hansen I felt desperate: in my madness I almost wished that Margot's injuries were more serious, to make her stay. —Where are you *going*? Margot protested from the bed, when I followed Teresa downstairs.

—I'll be back in a minute.

The landing light was on upstairs but it was dim in the hall, crowded with the designer furniture and antiques that Margot and Dickie had bought in another life, stacked with unopened boxes from the wine merchants; the walls were hung with paintings indecipherable in the dusk, too many for the small space. I hadn't tried to bring any order to this house since I'd come to live in it. I'd simply accepted its logic and routines, its chaos. —I'm sorry about Dickie, I said to Teresa, blundering after her into the porch. —My mother said he made a nuisance of himself.

She laughed and said that Dickie was a sweetheart. —He was never any trouble. I didn't mind him.

—I can't tell you how grateful I am for everything.

—Don't worry, no problem.

We weren't wearing our masks. I hadn't thought at first to put mine on in the emergency, and anyway I was indifferent just then to the possibility of contagion. I burst into tears and threw my arms around Teresa, burying my head in her softness and heat, feeling the resilience of her bust under the polyester housecoat, breathing in her unknown exotic smell—skin cream and sweat and cooking, cigarette smoke, traces of last night's perfume. This embrace felt momentous, as if a character had stepped out of my dreams to hold me. She was patting my back soothingly; I'm sure I was just another old woman to her, as crazy as my mother. If she held herself cautiously away from me, I don't think it was because of Covid.

—I'm so sorry, I said.

—You've had a shock. Don't worry.

—Just wait with me for a moment. I'll be all right in a moment.

I clung to her for a few seconds more, in the chill from the open front door. And then I let her go, there in the porch with its breath of damp doormat, its coat hooks still laden with Dickie's coats and cashmere scarves. He'd been quite a dandy when it came to his outdoor wear; a carved wood sculpture of a reclining nude wore one of his caps at a jaunty angle. Teresa hurried away; I heard her punch the buttons on the key safe next door. It was drizzling in the dark outside and a car sloshed past in the wet. I remembered from my time at school how little it took to set a day apart, surround it with happiness; perhaps one of the girls I worshipped gave me a biscuit left over from her break, or asked if she could copy my Latin homework. It was only later, when I transferred my worship to men, that everything grew complicated. But I was happy again that afternoon in lockdown, taking tea upstairs on a tray for myself and Margot. I had to hide my happiness from my poor mother, who was in pain while we waited for the paramedics. She was suspicious: *Why are you smiling?* And I knew it was ridiculous, because nothing had happened, nothing was going to happen. But I was thinking of Emma Bovary, staring at herself in the mirror after her tryst in the woods with Rodolphe, murmuring over and over, *I have a lover, I have a lover.*

Acknowledgements

Thank you as ever dear Jennifer Barth and Michal Shavit for looking after my stories, thank you dear Joy Harris and Caroline Dawnay for looking after me. And I owe such a debt of gratitude to Deborah Treisman, who published my first short story in *The New Yorker* more than twenty years ago. It was the kind of happy ending to all my early struggles with writing which would be too unconvincingly good to be true, if it hadn't happened in real life.

A NOTE ABOUT THE AUTHOR

Tessa Hadley is the author of three previous collections of stories and eight novels. She was awarded the Windham-Campbell Prize for Fiction, the Hawthornden Prize, and the Edge Hill Short Story Prize and has been a finalist for the Story Prize. She contributes regularly to *The New Yorker* and reviews for *The Guardian* and the *London Review of Books*. She lives in Cardiff, Wales.

A NOTE ON THE TYPE

This book was set in a version of the well-known Mono-
type face Bembo. This letter was cut for the celebrated
Venetian printer Aldus Manutius by Francesco Griffo,
and first used in Pietro Cardinal Bembo's *De Aetna* of
1495.

The companion italic is an adaptation of the chan-
cery script type designed by the calligrapher and printer
Ludovico degli Arrighi.

Composed by North Market Street Graphics,
Lancaster, Pennsylvania

Printed and bound by Berryville Graphics,
Berryville, Virginia

Designed by Betty Lew